TRANSFORMATION

Once out of sight of the inn, he stopped and stripped his borrowed clothes from him, rolling them in a bundle that he fastened against his neck so that it hung around his chest. Trembling a little from the night's chill, he willed the change to come to him. A moment later he stood, neither man nor beast but some terrible hybrid of the two, upright but furred, with a wolf's jaw but a man's brow, then he was loping along the road, powerful muscles propelling him at a mile-eating gait. His shoulder felt strong, but he still favored the one leg somewhat. It would be a long run.

Ainsy stood in the doorway until he disappeared into the swell of darker shadows beyond the perimeter of the inn's lights. She never saw the change, nor the wolf that he became. In her mind she pictured the man she knew, trudging along the road into the dark. . . .

FIREBIRD
WHERE FANTASY TAKES FLIGHT™

WOLF MOON

CHARLES DE LINT

FIREBIRD

AN IMPRINT OF PENGUIN GROUP (USA) INC

FIREBIRD
Published by Penguin Group
Penguin Group (USA) Inc., 345 Hudson Street,
New York, New York 10014, U.S.A.
Penguin Books Ltd, 80 Strand, London WC2R ORL, England
Penguin Books Australia Ltd, 250 Camberwell Road,
Camberwell, Victoria 3124, Australia
Penguin Books Canada Ltd, 10 Alcorn Avenue,
Toronto, Ontario, Canada M4V 3B2
Penguin Books (N.Z.) Ltd, 182-190 Wairau Road, Auckland 10, New Zealand

First published in the United States of America by Signet,
New American Library, 1988
Published by Firebird, an imprint of Penguin Group (USA) Inc., 2004

5 7 9 10 8 6

CIP DATA IS AVAILABLE UPON REQUEST FROM THE LIBRARY OF CONGRESS.

ISBN 0-14-240077-7

Printed in the United States of America

for my sisters
Kamé and Karin

WOLF MOON

First...

Since all is well, keep it so:
wake not a sleeping wolf.

—WILLIAM SHAKESPEARE
HENRY IV, PART 1.2

The music stopped.

The wolf paused at the abrupt silence, ears cocked, tongue lolling. His sides heaved as he panted for air. He stood at the base of a steep incline, concealed in a stand of cedar. His russet pelage, as red as a fox's, merged with the tree trunks and mulch of reddened branchlets underfoot so much that by remaining motionless, he was, to all intents and purposes, invisible.

Lifting his head, he sorted through the sea of odors that the wind brought him: pine resin, from higher up, and cedar; hare scent, old. His nostrils quivered. The wind came downhill, from behind. It took his own musty smell and sent it along his backtrail, offering no compensation for its betrayal. There were only sight and sound by which to measure the advance of his pursuers.

Sound came first, or rather, the hint of sound. Where branches should snap, or undergrowth be crashed with its passage, his bear-large stalker whispered through the forest. It seemed that the ground should vibrate under its relentless tred, but it moved as ghostlike and light-pawed as the wolf did himself. The wolf trembled with the need to run once more, but stayed to listen and watch, taking advantage of even this brief halt to recoup what he could of his depleted strength. Only when he saw the silvery bulk of the creature moving through the cedar and birch, did he dart from his hiding place to scramble up the bluff. As though timed to his motion, the music began once more.

The forest rang with it, deep chords that snaked their way uphill, entwining him with their unnatural harmonies. Inexorably, they worked their will on his consciousness—slowing his pace, sapping the purpose from his limbs, weighting his paws so that each step became an effort. It was harping, yet held in its biting chords the pitch and timbre of baying wolfhounds and the cries of hunters, the whistle and thud of a cast spear and the sharp winding of calling horns.

The grizzled guard hairs that saddled the wolf's shoulders hackled. It was only harping, he told himself, for all the chimerical associations that flooded his mind. Only harping?

He stopped again, slowed as much by the music as by a perverse need to catch a view of the pursuit, and studied his backtrail. The steep grade fell away in ridged folds of rocky ground, dressed with cedar and hemlock. Lower down, birch, aspen, and spruce vied for purchase with mossy granite outcrops jutting from the hillside like the grey bones of long-dead behemoths. In places, the roots of the trees twisted from the dark soil to wrap the rocks with knotted loops. A thick undergrowth of brush and year-old saplings choked the spaces between the trees. Ferns, dried and brown, swayed like broken fans under the drooping boughs. And then, through the crosshatch of the branches, as though summoned by his survey, he saw them.

The feragh came first, agile and supple-limbed for all its bulk, soft-stepping a path through the underbrush so that not one autumnal leaf seemed disturbed. Or did it simply, like some phantom, pass *through* the undergrowth? Its fur was a silvery grey, though the broad ursine features were streaked with darker markings like a mask. The same dark hair trailed from the beginnings of its mane, down along the shaggy ridge of its spine. It was as large as a bear and walked upright like a man. The scent that came to the wolf as the wind shifted was like a wolverine's—heavy and cloying.

It defied logic, should not exist. Even the forest appeared to sense it as something alien that was not to be abided. Did the trees not lean away from it as if to shun its presence, the ground shrink under its preternatural tred? The feragh belonged to the realms of myth. It should be bound in the words of a storyteller's tale, not walking the world, sharp-fanged and clawed; not real, with form and scent and substance, stalking him. But still it lived. The music gave it life. And it hunted. Hunted him.

As the feragh began its ascent, the harper stepped into view. He was tall and lean, clad in dark hunting leathers that clung tightly to leg and arm. His tunic was of a design more suited to courts and towns than to the forest. It was cut to his figure, with gathered folds at the shoulders and brocaded around the throat and sleeves. Silver embroidery threaded vines and flowers on each breast. The buckles on his boots and the tunic's buttons were silver as well, and sparkled.

When he caught sight of the wolf, he paused, staring uphill. His slender fingers tugged the weird music from a small journey-harp effortlessly, almost as an afterthought. The chords that filled the forest with their strength belied the instrument's size. The harp shone with an inner light and its dark wood gleamed, black as ebony. The forepillar, neck, and sounding board were unadorned, yet in that innocuous instrument throbbed the power that had raised a feragh from legend and set it on the wolf's trail.

There was magic afoot here, the wolf knew. Powerful magic against which he had no defense. Heavy though the feragh's scent was, smothering the man, the wolf could smell the sorcery. It burned in the music. It burned in the harper's features, highlighting his thin straight nose, planed brow, and gaunt cheek. It burned, too, in the feragh's eyes.

The wolf growled, deep in his chest. The creature was close. Too close. And almost the music had ensnared him. It forced the blood in his veins to pulse sluggishly, his head to droop with more than weariness. It bound his mind with lies of refuge and peace—did he only give himself over to it—but promised death in its underlying harmonies.

Snarling, the wolf turned to continue his own ascent, paws scrabbling for purchase in the thick carpet of pine needles and flat cedar leaves. His breath grew labored. Sharp jabs of pain accompanied each intake of air. At the summit he paused again. Foam flecked his lips and his tail hung limp, dragging on the ground.

He was no longer sure how long or how far the hunt had gone. The harping dulled his senses, weakened his limbs, and he could not find the strength to overcome it. He needed to strike out at his tormentor, to still the hateful music forever, but to reach the harper he must first face the feragh and in that action lay only death. He was unwilling to throw away his life. First the harper must be made to pay. That need sustained him more than simple survival.

The feragh was hellishly close. Its reek clogged the wolf's nostrils. The music fired his mind with scalding flames, numbing him. He willed his legs into motion. Powerful muscles bunched under his russet coat, but their main drive was gone. He staggered away from the summit's lip, half dragging himself through the trees. The wind brought him the scent of water and he came to a cliff's edge, high above a river.

He looked down at the white caps of the water as it roared between the rocks below. The sound of its passage was muted and lost under the harper's music. The weird harping was the only sound that existed now. He could hear nothing else. As he turned from the river to follow the cliff's ridge, the feragh broke from the trees behind and charged.

The wolf meant to leap under the sweep of the feragh's forelimbs, to strike for its throat, but his legs betrayed him. As the wind had. As the music did. He barely cleared the ground. The feragh's paw batted him out of the air and sent him skidding to the cliff's rim. Sharp pains lanced from his shoulder. As he moved, he could feel the raw wound tear. Dark blood clotted in his fur.

The feragh reared over him, blackening the sky. Saliva shone on the creature's long incisors, frothed in the corners of its open jaws. As the feragh dropped to attack, the wolf moved. With the last of his strength, before the creature could strike its final blow, he heaved himself over the cliff to plummet to the waters far below.

The harper arrived in time to see the wolf go over. He left off his harping and ran to the edge of the precipice to look down, ignoring the feragh's rancorous snarls at being thwarted. At first he saw only the white water as it rushed by, a hundred feet or so below. The rocks lifted from it like jagged teeth. He frowned. Then he saw something red bobbing downstream, watched it strike a boulder before the current dragged it under once more. He shrugged and ran his fingers through the feragh's mane, rubbing the soft spot under its ear. The bearlike face turned querulously to him.

"No. I fear the hunt's done for today."

The feragh rumbled a low bitter reply and the harper smiled.

"Another day," he said. His features grew thoughtful. "Though I find it strange that a simple beast could give us such a run. One might be led to think there was more to it than met the eye. And such a pelt! It would have made a fine addition to my cloak. I hear the winter is harsh in Penenghay and with a threadbare cloak. . . . Still. No matter. We've lost the beast now."

He sighed. Looking down at his harp, he pulled a sharp chord from its strings. At the sound of it, the feragh began to shimmer and grow insubstantial.

"I will say this, though," the harper added. "If it did survive, it won't escape us a second time."

By the time the chord's last echo died away, the harper stood alone on the clifftop. Except for some scratches on the stone underfoot and the scuffed mulch, there was no sign of the feragh. It had been summoned by harping; the same harping returned it to wherever it dwelled when the harper no longer had a use for it. It was his wild card when the stakes grew too steep. Yet it was his solace as well.

Swinging his instrument to his back, the harper kicked a stone over the edge of the cliff and watched it fall, vanishing in the storm of the white water as it dashed against the rocks. Then he turned to retrace his route through the forest.

Second...

"What do you make of this, then?" Brigg asked.

Tick pushed his way through the reeds and came to stand beside his cousin. The marsh ground squelched pleasantly under his boots and he wiggled his toes.

They were lowland kimeyn, these two. Marshdwellers. Smaller in stature than their mountain kin who shunned all but the heights of the ranges overlooking Penenghay Valley, they still shared the same blood. Atypical of their race, they stood just under four feet in their boots (though Tick was an inch taller), were thin but strong for their size, with narrow sharp-featured faces and unblinking round eyes. But while the mountain kimeyn were generally dark-haired, these two had unruly thatches of corn-gold hair, streaked with brown. Their tunics and leggings were of leather, discolored and patched in many places, and each had a small cap to hold down his hair. Tick's was berry red, while Brigg's was the yellow of goldenrod.

"Looks to be a man," Tick said. "Or what's left of one."

The object of their curiosity lay like a beached fish on

the riverbank, limbs splayed, face buried in the weeds, and naked as the day he was born. He was loose-limbed, with big hands and feet. Standing, he'd top the kimeyn by no more than a foot and a half. Gaunt ribs poked out, stretching the skin across his chest, and his hair, which was the red of an autumn maple, was plastered against his head. His features, when the kimeyn cautiously turned him over, proved to be strong. Homely, rather than handsome. But it was the dark bruises that discolored most of his torso and the raw wounds on his shoulder that drew their attention just now.

"Looks to be, aye," Brigg said. His nostrils crinkled and he shook his head. "But there was never a man with a scent like this one's."

"P'rhaps the water's washed his scent from him."

"P'rhaps it'll rain honey tonight."

Tick scrutinized the man carefully as an excuse to ignore the remark.

"Is he dead, do you think?" he asked at last.

"Hurt bad, seems. That shoulder needs looking after." Brigg looked upriver to where the Tattershall's waters cut through the hills. "The river's given him quite a spin. I wonder where he fell in and how far it took him before dropping him off here, on our doorstep, as it were."

Tick felt for a pulse at the man's throat. Standing, he wiped his hand dry on his tunic and looked at his cousin. "He's alive, sure enough. What should we do with him? Leave him?"

"Doesn't seem right."

"Doesn't," Tick agreed. "Still. He's just a man. Let them see to their own."

Brigg scratched his head, then busied his fingers with a tangle, tugging at it until the unruly locks were freed.

"Well?" Tick asked.

"Well yourself!" Brigg didn't like decisions. He had the tangle free and stuck his hands in the pockets of his tunic, poking a finger through the hole in the left one. He sighed heavily. "We can't just leave him."

"I suppose not. What's to do then? Take him home?"

Brigg shook his head. "We'll get the boat and take him to the Tinker. They can care for him there."

"But that's miles from here. Why so far? We could leave him in Hay-on-Pen, couldn't we?"

"And take our chances with all the menfolk crawling through the village?"

"To the Tinker, then," Tick agreed.

"To the inn, aye. So we'd best get going, hey?"

Tick nodded glumly, then brightened. "We can nick some ale while they're busy with him, couldn't we?"

Brigg grinned. "Why not? Some pie, too, if the mistress has been baking."

Tick rubbed his stomach. "Doesn't seem such a bad bargain, hey?"

"A right moon-send," Brigg agreed. "So let's hop to it."

They melted in among the reeds with the fluid swiftness that typified their race, returning in short order with a small coracle of tightly woven reeds that they launched into the Tattershall. A grass-rope line, running from one rounded bow and tied to a rotting stump near the water, kept the craft snug with the shore, bobbing slightly in the current. Tick looked critically from the coracle to their proposed load.

"What if he tips it over?" he asked.

"And what if he doesn't?" Brigg replied. "Now give me a hand."

Grunting with the effort, the two kimeyn lifted the limp body and laid him aboard. The coracle sank alarmingly under the weight, the gunwales topping the water by only six inches. They arranged the man in a curl at the bottom of the boat, knees drawn up to his chin. Brigg adjusted one of the arms, laying it over the knees, then gave his cousin a poke. Gingerly, Tick clambered aboard and the gunwales dropped another two inches.

"This might not be such a good idea," he said.

"Do you have a better?"

"No."

"I thought as much." Brigg cast off and boarded as well. The coracle dipped again. The tops of the sides were now less than an inch and a half above the water. The Tattershall, seeming to sense their predicament, proceeded to lap water over the gunwales and soon their passenger lay in a small pool of water. They propped his head under an arm to keep the water from his nose and mouth.

"Off we go then," Brigg muttered.

He took up a paddle, then cursed as the coracle hove to one side, sloshing water all over his leggings.

"Can you keep still?" he demanded.

"I thought my leg was going to sleep, all scrunched up as it was."

"If you tip us, I'll see that your noggin goes to sleep with the help of a couple of sharp raps from my knuckles."

Tick paddled in silence for a few moments, trying to think of a good retort, but came up blank. "How much ale do you think the boat could hold?" he asked at length.

"Far more than we'll be nicking. 'Ware that log!"

They both back paddled frantically, sloshing more water over the sides in the process, but managed to maneuver the coracle past the obstruction with only a scrape. Tick peered cautiously over the side to check for damage.

"Not a mark," he reported. "You know, I was thinking—"

"Just paddle," Brigg said.

He sighed and stared past his cousin's head, keeping a watch out for the turnoff that would let them bypass the village. If they managed this whole affair without a disaster of some sort, he'd consider himself lucky. And if they did, he'd pour a mug of the pilfered ale—a small one, mind you—on the moon's oak in thanks.

"Miss Ainsy! Miss Ainsy!"

Ainsy was cleaning out the hearth when she heard Wat's cry. She stood and wiped her hands on her smock before she thought of what she was wearing. Ruefully, she looked down at the two sooty smudges, one on either side of her hips, stark and black against the rust-and-yellow-flowered print.

"Oh, damn!" she muttered, and started across the common room to see what the commotion was about.

Her full name was Morain Tennen, though anyone who called her Morain had better be prepared to duck . . . quickly, and she was half owner of the Inn of the Yellow Tinker. The other half was owned by her uncle Tomtim, who spent the better part of every year outside the valley, following the trade of the inn's namesake. She was nine when her parents had died and Tomtim brought her to live at the inn. When Aunt Emma died three years ago, full responsibility for running the place had fallen squarely on her shoulders.

She was twenty-four now and still small for the size of her bones, rounded more than plump, and light on her feet. Her skin had kept most of its summer tan though her hair, a frizz of light brown that she kept braided while she worked, was beginning to show dark around the roots. Her eyes, large and expressive, were quick to laugh or flash with anger, more green than brown, with a scatter of gold flecks in the left one. They were her best feature, which wasn't to say she was unattractive. There was many a lad, from Hay-on-Pen and the farms round about, that would be eager to court her did she only give them half of a chance. It was just that the day-in-day-out duties of running the inn took their toll.

Her brow was creased with worry lines, more often than not, which gave her a somewhat harried look, and her lips often seemed set in a half frown, though it might be noted that her smile, when it came, lit the whole of her face, from dimpled chin to the sparkle in her eyes, and was well worth the wait. The summer had been a busy time, but winter was at hand now and with it came a drop in trade as well as a chance to relax. When Winden Pass was snowed in, effectively sealing the valley from the outside world, only the locals came by for their mug of ale and a chat, and that was mostly at the end of the week's work.

"Miss Ainsy!"

"Leave off your bellowing, you great lummox!" she shouted back. "I'm coming!"

She wondered what was causing the uproar. She had a hundred things she'd wanted to get done today and it seemed that every time she turned around something came up to keep her from them. She didn't even want to think about what Wat might have gotten up to. It was true that he was easily excited, but what could possibly get him so worked up today? They didn't even have one guest staying with them.

Unless it was the goats. If he'd let them out of their paddock again—broom and heather! He could bloody well chase after them himself, even if it took him the whole of the night to catch them and he missed his supper. But when she stepped from the inn's front door, she could see him down by the riverbank, leaping about on one foot. Had he drowned one of the goats? She broke into a trot, biting down a sharp remark.

They'd inherited Wat from a nameless journeyman and his wife who'd been passing through, stopped one night, and left before dawn without paying their bill. What they *had* left was their twelve-year-old son—not entirely dim, but not quite all there either. Tomtim had been all for chasing after the boy's parents, until Emma had her say.

"You'll do no such thing, Tomtim Tennen! The poor lad. Look at him. Would you take him back to folk such as they, when you know all they'll do is abandon him elsewhere? They may lack love, but we do not. He's here now, and it's here he will stay!"

And so he did. That was the same year that Ainsy came to the Tinker and the two of them had grown up like brother and sister. At twenty-seven, Wat was big and broad-shouldered, topping her by better than a head and a half, with a boyish face and a fourteen-year-old's mind in his grown man's body. A big lug, Ainsy might call him, but she loved him with all her heart. He was as kind-hearted a soul as could be found, gentle with the animals that were his responsibility, though shy with the inn's patrons. He slept in the barn all year-round, not because he had to, but because he couldn't bear to have his wards sleep alone. The donkey and goats, chickens and pigs, barn cats and his dog Stram—these were his closest friends.

He helped with the heavy work, that which she or the others couldn't handle on their own, and if he needed to be watched over more than most, that was more than balanced by his sweet nature. He could seem fierce as well—more than one fight in the common room had been stopped by calling him in—but that fierceness was all show. It was his size that intimidated the brawlers, and unless they were strangers, they knew better than to try their fists on him. Ainsy, never far from him when such occasions arose, swung a mean broom.

She was alone with him today. Tomtim was due home any day and how she longed to see his tinker wagon standing in its place by the barn, and Tomtim underfoot in the inn, long legs sprawled out before him, pipe smoke billowing up around his head. Tolly the stableboy had gone into town with Fion, who, along with Ainsy, doubled as cook, serving maid, and whatever else was needed.

They had taken the donkey and cart to the village early in the morning to lay in staples for the winter. Flour from Tadder's Mill—if it had been delivered to Comson's. Salt. Tea. Cloth. Anything else they needed, they either grew or provided for themselves. Ales and wines were brewed in the cellar. They had milk, cheese, and cream from the goats. Eggs from the chickens, though that broke Wat's heart. It was only because his memory was so short that he didn't exist entirely on a vegetarian diet.

Three times a year one of the pigs was butchered for bacon and ham and fat. They always sent Wat into the woods on an errand on those days. Hunters provided venison, duck, and quail. The garden offered grains and vegetables, herbs and some spices. The orchard gave them fruit—though only apples and pears. The forest provided berries and nuts. The bees honey.

As Ainsy crossed the road, she wished Tolly and Fion were back. There was no telling what Wat might have stirred up and she was too busy with her own work to keep a proper eye on him. He was out of sight now, having gone down to the river proper.

The land on the inn's side of the river was higher than that on the east side. They had the Tamwood behind them, while the opposite bank was nothing more than acres of marsh. So the drop, from the road to the riverbank, was steep. Ainsy scrambled down, then stopped dead in her tracks to stare at what lay at Wat's feet.

"Oh, Wat. What have you done?"

A naked man lay there, his body covered in yellow and blue-black bruises. His left shoulder was gashed as though some wild animal had clawed him and he was streaked with mud.

"I didn't do anything, Miss Ainsy." Tears welled up in Wat's eyes. Ever since Aunt Emma had died, she'd gone from simple Ainsy to Miss Ainsy in his mind. "I . . . I just found him is all. Didn't even touch him."

No, he couldn't have, she realized. The bruises wouldn't have come up that fast and there was no way Wat could have delivered the shoulder wounds. Besides, what would he have done with the man's clothes? She felt terrible for even having entertained the thought that Wat was responsible. But in the back of her mind she was always afraid of something like this happening. It came from watching him break up a fight in the common room, or seeing him carrying half a tree to the chopping block on his own. Gentle he might be, but he didn't know his own strength. And if he ever truly got angry with someone when she or one of the others weren't around . . .

"I'm sorry Wat," she said. She wiped a tear from his cheek and stood on her tiptoes to kiss him. "Of course you had nothing to do with it."

Wat sniffled and rubbed his eyes. Ainsy stared down at the man, feeling totally at a loss. Was he even alive? She knelt down beside him and, putting her ear to his chest, heard a weak heartbeat. Not dead, then. At least not yet. But what was she supposed to do with him? And how had he gotten here? He was too far from the water's edge to have been washed ashore. Besides, surely he'd have drowned if that had been the case. Wouldn't he?

"How did you find him?" she asked. "Did you see any-body else?"

Wat shook his head. "I was looking for Stram and then I just saw him like that and I called for you 'cos I didn't know what to do. I knew you were busy and all, but–"

"That's all right. It was right of you to call me. But how did he get here?"

Wat pointed beside the body. Tiny bootprints came and went from the water's edge.

"Kimeyn," he said seriously. "They must have left him here."

"Now don't start with that," Ainsy said. She looked at the bootprints and measured them in her mind. They *were* small. Not that she could give credence to Wat's ex-planation. The day she actually saw one of the Good Folk was the day she'd start believing in them. But that left only children, which didn't sit right either. Men with small feet? Perhaps. The bootprints sank deeply enough into the mud for that, except that children carrying the man's heavy weight would leave marks as deep.

Giving up, she stood and looked down at her smock. Soot *and* mud. Well, that was the least of her worries.

"Can you carry him back to the inn, Wat? And be gen-tle. Think of eggs."

Wat nodded. Proud to be of help, he lifted the man as carefully as though he were helping a newborn kid take its first few steps. When Ainsy was sure that he had his burden well in hand, she led the way back up to the road.

No sooner had she crossed it than she heard a crash from the direction of the inn.

"Arn above! Now what?"

She ran for the inn, letting Wat follow at his own pace. Skidding to a stop in the common room, she peered around, blinking as her eyes adjusted to the change in lighting. Nothing appeared to be disturbed. Feeling a pinprick of fear now—who could be here?—she made her way to the kitchen, walking cautiously. There she found the source of the noise, if not the culprit. The backdoor stood ajar, swinging silently on its oiled leather hinges. Strewn across the floor were a half-dozen pots and pans and—

"Damn! Damn!"

The rhubarb pie she'd baked for supper was gone. Who had taken it? She started to pick up the pans, then heard Wat in the common room.

"What shall I do with him, Miss Ainsy?"

"Throw him back in the river for all I care!"

She wished there was something she could take her frustration out on. Wat's face creased with confusion.

"Throw him back . . . ?"

Ainsy shook her head and kicked a pan. It skittered across the kitchen floor with a satisfying clatter. When she turned to Wat, her face was more composed. What to do with their uninvited guest? She didn't want to put him upstairs, where she'd be running up and down the stairs all night and day. That left Wat's unused room or. . . .

"We'll put him in Tomtim's room for today."

Wat nodded a little warily and Ainsy sighed.

"I'm not mad at you," she said. "It's just turning into one of those days. 'Bog a-fore, bog behind, and bog underfoot,' as Tomtim would say. You go on while I get some bandages."

On her way through the common room, she glanced at the bar to see ale dripping from the tap of one of the casks. There was a small puddle on the floor under the spigot.

"Did you steal the sheets from the beds while you were at it?" she shouted at the empty room. She shook a fistful of bandages in the air.

"Miss Ainsy?"

Wat stood in the passageway that led to their own quarters.

"I'm coming, Wat. But if I get my hands on the sods responsible for today's chaos, they'll rue the day they were born. *Did you hear me?*"

There was no answer. Only the growing concern in Wat's eyes.

"Who are you shouting at?" he asked.

"Myself," she said. "Unfortunately, only myself. Let's go see to our patient. Perhaps he'll shed some light on the mystery if he survives. Though with our luck he'll probably kick off in the middle of the night—after I've wasted the better part of the afternoon seeing to him, of course. Bah!"

She pushed past Wat and stomped down the passageway to Tomtim's room. Wat trailed along behind, shaking

his head and thankful that he wasn't the object of her
anger.

"He looks sort of interesting, don't you think?" Fion remarked. She drew the sheet back a bit and pulled a face
when she saw the bruises.

Ainsy tugged the sheet from her hand and tucked it
back up around her patient's chin.

"He's sick," she said, "so you might as well save your
charms for when he can appreciate them."

"A little touchy today, are we?"

Ainsy glared at her, but Fion smiled sweetly until she'd
charmed the flash from Ainsy's eyes. Born and raised
on a farm north of Pen-on-Water, her dad had, good-
naturedly but firmly, given her a choice five years earlier:
find work or he'd marry her off. With the three boys all
married and their wives living on the farm, there simply
wasn't room for his "twenty-three-year-old spinster,
more's the pity." Feeling that choosing one of her admir-
ers above the others would be unfair to the rest, she'd
opted for work and found it at the Tinker.

She was bosomy and wide-hipped, a half head taller
than Ainsy, dark-haired where the other was fair. She
wore her necklines low, her waists tight-laced, her skirts
flouncy. And though she wasn't nearly as loose-moraled
as she pretended to be, she loved to flirt.

"He looks like he fell down a mountain," Tolly said.

He stood with his hands in his pockets, leaning against

the door jamb. He was a distant cousin-by-marriage to Fion—"Very distant," Fion would say when she was fed up with him for one reason or another—who after being shunted from household to household when his parents had died, had finally found a permanent home at the Tinker. "We're all orphans of one sort or another," Fion had remarked once, "so we might as well stick together." Wat, delighted at the idea of having another brother and sister, never tired of repeating those words—especially in the middle of an argument.

Sixteen this summer, Tolly was tall and thin—more from his age than inherently, for just these past few months he had started to fill out. He kept his hair short, for it was curly as a corkscrew and impossible to manage when it was long, and proudly wore a light down on his chin and upper lip.

"Well," Ainsy said. "Now that he's been inspected by the both of you, perhaps we can leave him to his rest and go have our supper? Arn knows what took you so long to go to and from town. It's not as though Hay-on-Pen's on the other side of the mountains."

"We had to wait at Comson's for the flour. His driver stopped in at the Tager for a pint, it seems, and fell in with some cronies." Tolly pushed himself away from the door and set off down the hall. "Did you bake a pie?" he called back over his shoulder.

"I baked one," Ainsy replied, shooing Fion out the door and closing it softly behind them. "A nice rhubarb pie that someone pilfered while Wat and I were seeing to the amazing naked man."

Tolly stopped and turned an anguished face toward her. "Stole it?"

"The pie and some ale. Then they took the time to scatter some pots all over the kitchen floor as they were leaving."

"Did you catch them?"

"Did you see them hanging by their heels from the gate?"

Tolly stepped aside so that she could huff by him and rolled his eyes at Fion. "Well, now we know why Wat's so quiet," he said. "I thought it was because Stram took off into the woods this morn."

"It must come from her mother's side of the family," Fion replied. "Arn knows her uncle's a mild-mannered man."

"I think she's worried about Tomtim. He's never been this late before. She'll be unbearable if he doesn't show up before the pass is snowed shut."

"Tomtim will make it, never fear. That old tinker'd die if he didn't have the inn to laze about in all the winter." Fion grinned. "Where else could he have it so easy?"

"Are you two coming?" Ainsy demanded from the kitchen. "Or do you plan to gossip in the hallway all night?"

"We're coming," Tolly said. He turned to Fion. "If it's 'tater stew again. . . ."

Fion wagged a finger at him. "Don't complain unless you're willing to do better yourself. Oh, cheer up!" she added. "One long face is enough for tonight. Behave and I'll share an opentie with you that'll drive the girls wild. I saw you in Hay-on-Pen today, mooning about like a sick calf, your tongue clove to the roof of your mouth. You'll have to do more than grin like a farmer, me lad. It's the first thing you say that's the most important."

"Can we practice after supper?"

"Practice? And have Ainsy take it out of my hide?" Fion shook her head. "No thanks. Talk's all we'll do. Now come on, before she comes looking for us, thinking we're bussing in the hall here or something."

Third...

Kern awoke in a cold sweat. He tore himself from his dreams, but although he left them behind in whatever place it is that dreams have life, the memory of them was still too immediate. His body was charged with adrenaline. Residuals of the dreams—bloody fragments of savageness that shocked him—left trails behind, like the traces a tel-smoker sees when he is high.

The feragh had been most prominent. It attacked him time and again, staggering in its violence, clawing at his eyes, shredding his wolfshape as though it were only so much paper wrapping, the slavering jaws closing inexorably around his furred throat. His pelage was wet and sticky with his own dark blood. A heartstopping cry rang in his ears, that only later he knew as his own. And undercutting it all, layering a cruel harmony against the feragh's savagery, was the harping. It cut at his soul, cold and distant, yet as immediate and piercing as a blade of hot fire.

A cool hand touched his fevered brow and he twisted

under it as though he'd been stung. He floundered in bed-sheets, snarling as his shoulder hit the floor. He snapped his eyes open, but a red wash of pain flooded his sight, blinding him. When it cleared, he was crouching against a wall, legs and arms trapped in folds of cloth, his lips pulled back to bare his teeth for all that he was still in manshape. He saw a dark-haired woman standing by a bed, her eyes registering a curious mixture of surprise and amusement.

"For someone who was near death yesterday," Fion said, "you're awfully spry today."

He made no reply. His eyes narrowed to slits as he watched her, nostrils widening as he recorded her scent, searched for others. In times of stress, his lupine instincts tended to rise to the fore. Though his shoulder throbbed with pain, no sign of it showed on his features.

"Not even a name?" Fion shrugged and called over her shoulder, "Ainsy! Your patient's returned to the land of the living!" Then she warned Kern, "You'd best be in bed by the time she comes or she'll scold the hide off you— what hide your own misadventures have left you, that is." As she took a step toward him, he backed up farther against the wall. "Oh, come on. I won't hurt you. She's going to think I tried to ravish you or something."

Still he watched her, silent and wary, appearing for all the world like some trapped animal. He seemed to shimmer before Fion's widening eyes, from man to beast to man. The first suspicions of fear began their eerie tiptoe up her spine and she began to wish she'd called for Wat as well. There was something comforting about his size at a time like this. She took a step back herself, wondering at what she'd seen—or thought she'd seen.

Ainsy bustled into the room.

"Arn above! What's going on?"

"Not what you think," Fion replied. "It's just that your amazing naked man has turned out to be an amazing wild man." She tried to instill levity into the situation, but her heart continued to thud uncommonly loud to her ears.

"You mean he—"

"Hardly. But . . . well, look at him."

Ainsy did. He was crouched against the wall like a fox at bay, preparing to make its last stand against the hounds. Sly and clever Reynard, reduced to his basic need for self-preservation. For the first time since Wat had found him, she could see his eyes. She shivered to look into them. They were green as a cat's, slitted and . . . wild was the only description that sprang to mind. Broom and heather! What had they let into their home?

She found her fingers curling at her side, reaching for the handle of the broom that she hadn't thought to bring. For a long moment tension crackled thickly in the air, feeding on their silence. Then the man appeared to relax. The fierce blaze in his eyes withdrew into a spark, became less bestial.

"Who are you?" he asked. His voice was husky and much deeper than Ainsy had expected from his size. "Where am I?"

Fion was the first to find her tongue. "We might ask you the same—about the who, that is. We know the where."

"I. . . ."

He fumbled awkwardly with the sheets and came across the bandages that bound his shoulder wound. As he looked down at it the last vestiges of . . . power? wildness? . . . deflated. Ainsy's own unaccountable fears subsided, replaced with curiosity and another feeling that she could neither put name to nor ignore. Pity for his hurts and helplessness? Him helpless? Wounded he might be, but he looked anything but helpless.

"My name is Kern Kindregan," he said, addressing her. He still fingered the cloth of his bandage and spoke with an element of self-reproach in his voice. "It seems you've helped me and received poor thanks in return."

"I'm Ainsy Tennen. And this is Fion."

"Well met, ladies." His sudden grin was infectious and Ainsy found herself smiling back. "Tell me, where did you find me?"

"You were on the riverbank—by the bridge. Just lying there in the mud. Can you remember what happened? Were you attacked?"

"No. I was . . . swimming. I guess the current proved too strong for me. The last thing I can remember is the sudden rush of the water and a big rock rearing up at me from out of it."

Ainsy and Fion exchanged glances. Swimming with winter almost upon them and the river swollen with autumn rains? Well, there was a saying in the valley, that all who lived beyond the mountains were more than a little mad. Kern attempted to stand up, but found it difficult to manage with the sheets entwined about him.

"Not so fast!" Ainsy cried, some of the usual sharpness returning to her voice.

He tripped and she lunged forward, grunting under his sudden weight.

"If you open that shoulder again. . . ."

She let him lean on her and steered him to the bed. As she straightened the sheets about his prostrate form once more, she noticed that his bruises were far less discolored than they had been yesterday. The least of them were already gone. The worst were no more than dark marks, tinged with yellow. He blushed at the touch of her hands, and though Ainsy didn't notice, Fion turned her head and smiled to herself.

"A little cold to be swimming, isn't it?" Ainsy asked.

"Well, when you're hot and dusty from the road, you don't really think about whether the water's cold or not."

"I suppose. Where was it? I'll send someone to fetch your clothes. You're in no shape to get them yourself."

"I'm not sure. There was a cliff that I climbed down. . . ." He shrugged, wincing with the movement.

Again the women looked at each other. If he'd been washed downstream—as he had to have been—the river must have borne him for leagues. The nearest high ground with cliffs overlooking the river was fifteen miles or so up the Tattershall. And how, Ainsy asked herself, did rocks tear the flesh like an animal's claws?

She looked down at Kern, trying to see what was hidden behind the affable expression he wore like a mask. She wanted to feel good about him—Arn knew why, except there was something about him that attracted her. But she couldn't shake the memory of how he'd looked when she'd come into the room. Savage. Who was he besides a name and a collection of cuts and bruises? She sighed and made a dismissing motion with her shoulders. If he wouldn't enlighten them, they'd be hard put to force him. Still, the curiosity remained, nagging at her with the same persistence of the big crow that had been after the corn all this summer.

"Did you come from the north or south?" she asked.

"South."

"You didn't see a tinker wagon along the way, did you? Two-horsed, the wagon painted yellow and red, though the paint's chipped and faded. An old man driving?"

Kern shook his head. "I didn't come through the pass. . . ." he began, then shut his mouth firmly. He could tell by their expressions that it had been the wrong thing to say.

"You came over the mountains?" Fion asked.

"But that's impossible!" Ainsy said.

Impossible? Not in wolfshape, carrying a small pack in his jaws. They'd been difficult to assay, those mountains, but not impossible. He was here, wasn't he? But that wasn't something he could explain. He passed a hand over his forehead, feigning a dizzyness he didn't feel. Through hooded eyes he watched the expressions on their faces change—from disbelief to an understanding that it was his fever that made him talk as he did.

"You'd better rest," Ainsy said firmly. "Do you feel up to some broth?"

"Please."

Rest? He could use some rest, though not nearly as much as they might think. He wished he knew what condition he'd been in when they'd found him. His metabolism was such that wounds healed quickly—far more quickly than they might with someone not like him. A shapechanger. His tissues were highly regenerative. His bones were much more pliable than theirs—for flexibility was important when one changed from man to wolf. Without it, the transformation would be as painful as it had been when the ability first surfaced.

But that was neither here nor there at the moment. How badly had he been hurt? He'd seen the question in Ainsy's eyes as she'd studied his bruises. He dredged the feragh up in his mind and tried to recall the damage of its blow. He'd been feverish then as well and now his recollection was poor. The feragh's swiping blow, the fall and hitting the water's surface, sinking like a rock when the air was knocked from his body, the rocks as the current dragged him downstream . . . and through it all the harping.

The creature. The harping. They brought the harper to mind. A rush of cold anger passed through him, stark and grim as the icy winds that come in winter. He hid the flare of emotion, trying to keep his features mild. It was difficult with that anger raging inside.

"Just lie back," Ainsy was saying. "The broth'll take a few moments to heat up."

Kern nodded and watched them leave with mixed emotions. They were good people—not like the other one in his dark hunting leathers. Their scent was clean, like freshly mown hay, like honeysuckle and lilacs. They wore their feelings openly, with no secrets hidden behind them, except for those that every woman had.

His lupine senses reached out, investigating the surroundings beyond the confines of the room. It would be nice to live in a place like this.

From smell and sound he judged he was on a farm of some sort—perhaps an inn. Remote, probably. Quiet, mostly. Peaceful, surely. He sighed and looked about the room.

Besides the bed on which he lay, the room presented a chair by the window—leather-bound and comfortable looking. A crude dresser stood across from the bed. It had two drawers, the bottom one a little warped, so that it couldn't close completely. A large brass candlestick perched on the top, its fat candle the creamy color of a mushroom stem. The third wall had a small bookshelf leaning against it, half full of leather-bound volumes. Beside it was the door. Above it a watercolor of a riverscape in a wooden frame with ornate curlicues. There was another above the bed, obviously the work of the same artist. (Someone who lived here?) It showed a woodland scene—a dainty doe poised in the umbrage of the forest's outermost trees.

Lying back, he imagined the room as his own, that he lived here, working at this farm/inn, had friends, if not family at least close ties, companionship. Then he imagined the woods. He smelled the dank forest door, felt the undergrowth comb his fur, the wind bringing the world to his nostrils, jays and ravens and squirrels quarreling in the trees above, somewhere a rabbit thumping its hind paw. Closing his eyes, he half dozed, unable, or unwilling, to decide which life held more appeal.

In the farm/inn environment, the wolf side of him would be fettered, trapped in manshape, unfree. And when they discovered his secret, as sooner or later they must, all earned friendship would die. As it always had. But in the forest he was alone too. The wolf packs shunned him for his strangeness—for the very humanity that men could not see once they learned his secret. But which was he? Man or beast? It was an old argument, that could no more be resolved today than the hundred other times he'd worried at it.

"What do you think of him?" Ainsy asked Fion as they made their way to the kitchen.

Through the open door they could see Wat playing with Stram. The dog's barks were strident and excited—as though he'd missed his master as much as his master had missed him. Ainsy wondered why he'd spent the night be-wooded then. Probably started off on some mad chase, one scent leading to another until he was miles from home. Got lost, more than likely, knowing Stram. But at least he was back now and Wat was happy.

"I think he took a couple of good whacks on the head, is what I think," Fion said. "Over the mountains! What does he think he is? A goat?"

Ainsy shook her head. "But there's something intriguing about him, that's for certain. More than just a knock on his head. Odd . . . but intriguing." She looked at Fion with a curiously fanciful expression in her eyes.

The other woman smiled inwardly and simply shrugged, saying nothing. Far be it from her to nip even the smallest interest in the bud. She had never met anyone so decidedly innocent in the ways of the heart as Ainsy. It came with responsibility, Fion supposed, though with a rapscallion like Tomtim for an uncle—if half his tales could be believed—surely Ainsy had her fair share of a tinker's passion for romance somewhere in her blood? She certainly had a tinker's disposition—as changeable as the winds themselves.

And it wasn't as though she was unattractive. She just never gave anyone a chance. She was more the spinster than Fion could ever be—charming with children, animals, and friends, but never taking time out for a little romance. What was life without the odd tryst under the oak at midnight? Damnably dull, is what!

Looking at Ainsy now, Fion thought, Perhaps the time's come. Now if only this Kern wasn't so . . . disreputable. Of course that was unfair. They knew next to nothing about him. He could be a lord's son, for all they knew. A lord himself, even.

"I think he's an outlaw," Ainsy said. "He has the look of a loner about him and he seems to be hiding, or running from something."

Fion remembered the feral look about him, crouched against the wall, the wild lights in his eyes, and saw that Ainsy was remembering too. An outlaw? It was a romantic thought. And a promising one. Not that he was an outlaw, but the romance. What with her talks with Tolly, and now this, she was becoming a regular little matchmaker.

"But he seems to be a good man. Perhaps he was wrongly accused or . . . oh, I don't know."

Now we're heading straight into the makings of a ballad, Fion decided. A good man? He seemed nice enough, if a touch mad. Over the mountains, indeed! And

swimming at this time of year? Again she went back—
thinking of that moment when he'd seemed to change before her eyes. Vague tales told at her dad's knee stirred
uncomfortably in her. Her father's farm bordered the
Tamwood north of Hay-on-Pen. He knew all the forest
tales and could convincingly relate the adventures and
perils of men who had met those strange beings that were
still supposed to haunt the woods. *Too* convincingly.

Images swam up from her subconscious like the slow
bubbles of a stew just before it boils. Kimeyn and bogeys.
The Green Man. Jack o'the Oak. The wild man of the
woods. And wasn't red hair a sign of feyness? Kern had
red hair. . . .

She had the sudden desire to warn Ainsy to go easy,
but knew she couldn't. If she said something now, it
could spoil everything. And besides. . . . She shook her
head, amused at the turn her thoughts had taken. She'd
seen a man startled out of a fevered sleep, his eyes still
haunted by whatever strange phantasms his delirium had
delivered to him, and she let her mind go wild with con-
jectures that were patently ridiculous when examined
with the smallest grain of reason.

"I promised to help Tolly with the pigs," she said. "I'll
leave you to look after our amazing wild man."

Ainsy frowned. "Kern," she said. "His name's Kern."

"Why, so it is."

Fion winked and flounced out of the kitchen.

Ainsy watched her go and shook her head. There were

times when Fion baffled her. She was Ainsy's elder by only four years but sometimes it seemed that the gulf separating them was decades wide. They were the best of friends, yet some things they simply couldn't see eye to eye on. She stood thinking of it for a long moment before remembering what it was that had brought her to the kitchen in the first place. Stepping into the walk-in pantry, she scooped a large ladle of cooled broth into a small iron pot and hung it over the fire.

Perched on the foot of the bed, Ainsy watched her patient spoon up his broth with the satisfaction of a cook seeing someone enjoying the fruits of her labors. She studied him surreptitiously, her hands folded primly on her lap, and reconsidered her earlier impressions. She could see little odd about him, except for his hair. Red was an uncommon hair color in the valley. And as for his wildness, there wasn't a hint of it left.

"You could use some clothes, " she said. "Something of Tolly's should fit you, though you'll have to roll up the sleeves and cuffs. I could stitch them for you."

Kern smiled. "I'd be grateful, but I don't want to cause any more trouble than I already have."

"It won't be any trouble."

"Are you sure?"

She shrugged. "You're not planning to wear a sheet, are you?"

"A loan then. Until I get my own back."

Taking the bowl from him, she set it beside her on the bed, thinking of what he'd just said.

"Kern. The nearest cliffs are twenty miles from here. Are you sure you were swimming in the Tattershall?"

"There were cliffs. I'm not certain of what river it was."

"The Tattershall starts in Snowberry Lake and runs through the Torenban Mountains, the Gwenwood, and the marshes, before joining the Penwater at Hay-on-Pen." She drew it out on the blanket as she spoke. "Where it cuts through the mountains, there are terrible rapids. And when it hits the marshes, there's hardly any current at all. How could the river have brought you all the way?"

"I wasn't exactly in top form at the time," Kern said mildly.

"Wat said the kimeyn brought you. There were very small footprints around your body—the size a child might make."

"Wat's the fellow who found me?"

Ainsy nodded. "He wants to meet you. I'll bring him in to see you later on. He gets a little rambunctious, and you still need your rest."

"I'd like to meet him. I owe him my life."

"But about those footprints. How *did* you get to the riverbank?"

"I owe you my life as well."

Two things made Ainsy uncomfortable—being complimented and being thanked. She felt her neck redden, the heat spread to her cheeks, and looked away to stare awkwardly at her shoes. There was still mud on them from yesterday's moment by the river.

"Where are you from?" she asked, to break the silence that was growing up between them. If he wouldn't talk about how he'd come to the riverbank, she'd get him to talk about something else. She liked the sound of his voice. "And what do you do when you're not lolling about half dead in the mud?"

Kern grinned. "I'm from Urthin, originally. But that was many years ago."

Almost another lifetime, he thought. It *was* another lifetime and it had belonged to someone else, not the person he was now. And now? How could he even begin to explain what he was? He turned his gaze to Ainsy and tried to shake free the feelings that were beginning to take root in him. There was something about her that made him want to lay bare his soul to her. He wanted to build a trust between then, but knew in his heart that it couldn't be.

There had been another woman, in a small village that he could no longer remember the name of. But though the village was forgotten, she wasn't. Tera. But he didn't remember her for the love that had been between them. He remembered her as a warning of what had happened when he allowed himself to love another. For all the years that had passed since his being with her, he could never forget the revulsion and fear in her face when she had come to understand what he was. If there hadn't been a storm that night, he would never have escaped the hunters and their dogs. . . .

He had never harmed her, nor any in her village. But she hadn't seen that. She had seen only a monster, known only terror, and called down the hunters on him. The blacksmith's shop was busy that night, melting down silver for arrowheads—the silver that was poison to his kind. By the time they had set out, he was long gone, the heavy rains wiping clean his trail.

Luck alone had saved him. Certainly not his ludicrous attempt to be trusted, to be accepted for what he was. He did not plan to repeat that error. He had not repeated it for all those years. He would certainly not repeat it with the woman who sat now on the end of the bed, who'd tended to his wounds and watched him now with an echoing warmth in her eyes, who set the blood to pounding in his veins. The instinct for self-preservation had grown too strong. And he didn't ever want to see in another's face what he had seen in Tera's.

The shapechanger's gift—or curse, depending on one's viewpoint—had come to him when he turned thirteen, hard on the heels of puberty. They were connected in some way, he knew, as though whatever gave the gift knew that a babe or toddler would be too young to deal with the problems attendant upon the ability—though such problems arose more from the reactions of others than from the gift itself. But, in retrospect, it wasn't that much easier on a naive farmer's son who knew little more than tending crops and livestock.

His sexuality had awakened first. It happened at night when he was alone in his room, his manhood rising between his legs like a small sapling. It wasn't until years later that he heard men joking about the tree of life. One moment it was no more than an organ with which to relieve his kidneys. Then his hand touched it, curiosity triggered a rhythm, and his fingers and bedclothes grew sticky with his ejaculation. It was innocently done. But young as he was, with no understanding of what had happened, the moment had fired him with a burning shame.

The shapechanging brought shame, too, but the terror of it was stronger. The pain of that first time remained through all the years that followed. His bones were still pliable, due to his youth, and remained so, the more he changed, but that first time as they contorted, the stretch and twist of limbs and skin, the wrenching as he became something else, something not human, had nearly shattered his mind.

He'd been alone in the holding that night, which was all that aided him in keeping the gift a secret from his parents as long as he had. He'd twisted in the bedclothes that night—furred and clawed, a gangly wolf pup, lean and gaunt-chested, but with power in his young muscles. Fighting free of the blankets, he'd rolled to the floor, tried to stand as a man, been unable to comprehend why he couldn't. Beyond the window, the fields called to him, be-yond them the forest. And above it, strongest of all, the moon. Gentle mother, watching down on that first change, full and silver above his parents' holding. When understanding finally came to him, he saw himself as a creature of legend, and whispered a name in the loneli-ness of his thoughts. Werewolf. Nightstalker.

That first night had held both terror and joy. Terror at the change, but it could not erase the joy of the loping run under the night skies, the wind in his fur, the darkness filled with a hundred scents and odors. He'd pitied his par-ents that night, pitied any woman or man that couldn't know/feel/sense what he did. But in the morning, his se-cret grew into a burning guilt. And then he knew another face of fear—that he would be discovered, that he was evil, that he would be slain.

He wondered, in later years, how many others had de-luded themselves in the same fashion when the gift first came to them. Did they curse it as he had? Curse it and yearn for it, a constant seesaw of self-hate and a wolf's fierce pride? Did they fear the full moon as he had? Gentle mother, Arn above, who gifted her furred children with night's cloak? Or did they go on to learn that the change could come at will, that it was not bound to the moon and her aspects? Did they come to find the trans-formation both easy and pleasurable, or were they locked into the lies of it, their subconscious blaming the moon and their changes coming only during the three nights of her fullness?

For that was all the werewolf was, he came to understand. A shapechanger locked in the lies of legend and false histories that told them they were evil, that the change could not be controlled, that when they changed they must strike out at those who did not have the curse, as savagely as the feragh that had hunted him yesterday. They thought the moon was the trigger—for all that they could change anytime, day or night—looked on the gift as a curse and shunned the company of their fellowmen. Unless they were hunting.

He knew better, though how the knowledge had come to him, he wasn't sure. Yearning to change one night when the moon wasn't full, and finding himself in lupine form? Or had it been in the day, walking alone in the woods and longing for that sleeker shape that understood the forest better than a man did his own home?

Still the knowledge had not stopped him from becoming as much of a loner as any of them. How could it be elsewise? Too much the wolf to live among men. Too much the man to live among wolves.

He was driven from home when his parents discovered what he'd become. He could still hear the terrible arguments as each cursed the other's bloodline. He had tried to tell them of the joys, that it was not evil, but when he saw his father taking a silver candlestick into town, he'd seen the futility of it and departed that same morning, never to return.

Since then he had wandered, the very act of moving from town to town becoming a way of life. He'd journeyed with tinkers and peddlers, but in the end journeyed mostly on his own. Only then could he know true freedom. Only then could he travel in whatever shape he wished—the man when he moved through settled country, the wolf with the small pack in his jaws, when he traveled the wilds.

The most important lesson he had learned after leaving his parents' holding, was that the world was wide beyond his imagining and held a vast wealth of knowledge and experience, that the small corner he'd known all his short life, was but the barest scrapings of it. He'd had only one objective in his life then, and that was to learn and experience as much of the world's wonder as he could in the years still left to him. Not to garner wisdom as a bee might honey, or to miser his gold. But simply to realize it. The greatest crime of all, to his way of thinking, was to turn one's back on those wonders. For with the closeness of friendship denied him—whether it be with men or wolves—it was all that remained for him.

"What if I can't find something nice to say?" Tolly asked.

"How so?"

"Well, to compliment them. Like you were telling me last night."

Fion shook her head. "If you can't find something good to say about a girl, why in Arn's name would you want to meet her?"

"I don't know."

They were spreading hay in the pigpen after having cleaned it of its manure. Behind the barn was a tall pile of it that still had to be spread over the garden after it was turned for the winter.

"I think pigs shit more than any other animal in the world," Fion had muttered as they shoveled it out.

Wat was playing with Stram, staying near to his wheelbarrow in case they had another load for him, whether it be pig manure to add to the pile or hay for the pen. Stram was a gawky mongrel—a "bedamn" Fion called him, meaning a mix of too many breeds for any one to be prominent. It was a term she'd picked up from a southern merchant who'd stayed at the inn two summers ago.

Stram was a shag of brown hair, long-legged and snubspouted, looking more like a small haystack with legs than a proud member of the canine family. He loved to explore the woods, staying away for a day at a time every other week or so, as he had yesterday, much to Wat's continuing distress, returning, more often than not, with a mouthful of porcupine quills, burrs matted in his fur, or reeking of skunk.

"Ainsy's in a good mood today," Tolly remarked.

"Maybe she has good reason to be," Fion replied with a grin.

"You mean the stranger?"

"His name's Kern, it appears. Kern Kindregan. And he's suitably mysterious and therefore romantic. I left the two of them mooning over each other, though neither of them'd ever admit it, I'm sure."

"I find that hard to believe."

"And why's that?"

"Well . . . Ainsy?"

Fion laughed. "Maybe there simply wasn't anybody interesting enough before. There's more to life than bussing under the oak."

"That from you?"

Fion pitched a forkful of hay in his direction. "Watch your tongue, you great dunt-about! You'd be better off thinking with your head than with what's between your legs."

"Hey!" Tolly brushed the hay from him and sneezed.

"Well, I for one am glad for her," Fion said. "Sudden and all, it'll still do her some good, so long as he stays around for a bit. Unfortunately, he appears to be somewhat of a wanderer, more's the pity."

"But *Ainsy?*"

"Still waters run deep and all that. Now leave off, or I'll let you finish the rest of this yourself. I can think of better ways to spend my afternoon than spreading pig shit over the garden."

"I'm sure you can," Tolly said, and ducked as another forkful of hay was flung at his head.

~~~~

"Where's Urthin?" Ainsy asked.

"Quite aways west of here. You'd find it an odd place, I think. It's mostly lowland—at least the part I'm from—with the highest hill being no taller than the pines in these Mountains. Farmland, mostly. I left it when I was very young."

"What did you do then?"

"Wandered mostly." Kern shrugged. "It's not such a bad life, though it's not so free and easy as some might think. Summer and fall are the best. The woods give both shelter and food, and if a man starves, it's only because he was born blind and stupid. It's harder in the winter. Then I usually try to find a holding to work in until the spring. Often I can get hired for the harvest and simply stay on till the snows break and the weather changes. This year I had some coin saved up—enough to see me through the winter, I'd thought—and meant to travel as far as it would last me." He smiled ruefully. "It didn't last me very long, it seems. My coin pouch was in my pack and the stars alone know where that is now."

"You could stay here, if you'd like," Ainsy said, somewhat startled at her own boldness. But once it was said, there was no taking it back. She didn't want to take it back. Her heartbeat quickened as she waited for his answer. "Of course you'd have to help out around the place, though there's not a great deal needs doing in the winter months."

Kern was sorely tempted. He met her eye and was touched by her warmth. She was a lovely woman, with quirksome moods. Betimes she seemed like a stern dame; other times her eyes sparkled and she was a young woman, kindly hearted and full of fun. He'd already discovered how her smile brightened her face, and worked at keeping it tugging at her lips.

"It's kind of you to offer," he said. "But you know next to nothing of me, and rather than having you bound to something you might regret all too soon, why don't we wait a few days and see how it goes?"

Strangely disappointed, Ainsy nodded. Though, as a glimmer of understanding came to her, her disappointment wasn't so much strange as uncommon. It was something new, this emotion tugging at her heart that soft-stepped through her with an unfamiliar tread, curiously sweet, but frightening too. For Kern was right. She *did* know next to nothing about him. There was too much that was a mystery about him, too many secrets locked behind those green eyes.

But that mystery, that difference, was what drew her to him in the first place. It wasn't so much that he was a pleasing change from the local lads, which he was. She was used to all manner of different folk stopping by the inn on their way through the valley, though none had come before with only the—she smiled—bare essentials as he had. No. What it was, was a sense of the woods and the river and the mountains that he brought with him.

Sitting on the bed and talking with him was like taking a walk through a forest. There was that same . . . stillness in him.

"Have you never traveled?" Kern asked suddenly. "Or just wanted to know what lay over the next hill?"

Ainsy frowned at the thought. "Me? With an inn to run? Bad enough that Tomtim's got the itch. If we were both traipsing off into the wild blue yonder, the Tinker'd tumble down from neglect."

"Tomtim . . . Is that who you were asking me about earlier?"

"He's been due for a few weeks. I expect him any day."

"You're worried about him, aren't you?"

Ainsy stared down at her feet for a long time without answering. Clicking her heels together, she watched flakes of mud fall off her shoes to freckle the floor.

"It seems I'm always worried about something or other," she said at last, not looking up to meet his gaze. "I get tired of it sometimes. I try to not let things bother me, but . . . well, I suppose it's the tinker blood. It comes out in my temper instead of a wanderlust. I wonder which is better?"

"I'm not the one to ask," Kern replied, trying to get her to smile again.

"I suppose not. But Tomtim's never been this late before. He can be a nuisance—hanging about in everybody's way all winter when he's not out in the barn hammering in his smithy—but I don't know what I'd do if he never came back. It's got to happen someday, I suppose. He's not getting any younger and the world's as wide as ever, but—"

"He'll come soon," Kern said, but knew the words didn't have much weight to them. How could he say when her uncle would come?

Ainsy sighed and took a deep breath. The moment had been magical until they'd started talking about wanderings and Tomtim. She knew now that Kern would be no different from her uncle. The road would always call him. Even if he stayed a few weeks, or the winter, with them, he'd be off again, no matter how she pretended otherwise to herself. Only why were her feelings so strong this time, whereas they'd never been before?

Kern sensed the mood shift and worked hard at erasing the worry lines from Ainsy's brow. He launched into a long, implausible story that soon had the corners of her mouth tugged up in a smile. By the time the tale was done, she was sitting up on the bed facing him, legs tucked up under her, her face awash with laughter. She forgot her misgivings and took Fion's advice for a change. "Go with the moment," the dark-haired woman never tired of telling her. So this time she had. Now all too soon the morning was gone and it was time to get things ready for lunch. Wat, if no one else, would be sitting at the table waiting for her.

"What would you like for lunch?" she asked Kern.

"Whatever you're having. If you could bring me those clothes you were speaking of earlier, I'll get up and—"

"Not a chance! Perhaps for dinner. I'd like to clean that shoulder of yours and put some fresh bandages on it before you're up and about."

Kern gave an exaggerated sigh, but she wouldn't be swayed. The stern dame flashed in her eyes and he held up his hands in mute acquiescence. When she left, he lay back to stare at the ceiling. At that moment he'd have traded anything to be a mundane. He turned the word over in his mind. To a shapechanger it meant not so much plain as normal. Before he'd come to grips with his gift— when he had still considered it a curse—there were many times he'd wished he was as much a mundane as most folk. That had been years ago and he didn't think he'd ever feel like that again. But raising Ainsy's face in his mind's eye, hearing again her voice, that feeling was a sharp ache, deep inside.

That evening, the ache grew only stronger.

He sat at the big table in the kitchen, feeling somewhat scruffy in Tolly's clothes, which were, indeed, a good size too big for him. Having been duly introduced to the others, he bided quietly, letting the conversation wash about him. They were kind to him, each of them seeking to make him feel at home in his or her own way, which only heightened Kern's feelings of alienation. If-only's and what-ifs paraded through his mind, but each time he took one in hand and said, Yes, perhaps I could, the darkness beyond the kitchen window called out to him. The darkness, and the forest beyond it, and he remembered the wolf that shared the flesh of his mortal frame.

Sighing, he mopped up the last of his stew with a chunk of home-baked bread. The conversation was centered on Wat's dog and what exactly it did on its extended excursions into the forest.

"Like as not," Fion remarked, "he's got some dainty vixen he courts. Brings her table scraps and what-not in hopes of winning her over. I won't be surprised to see some very strange foxes in the woods come spring."

Kern joined in the general laughter. He looked from face to face around the big table and, setting his own concerns aside as best he could, tried to relax. The company was good. He had a full stomach and a large mug of steaming tea at his elbow. What more could a man ask for?

"You shouldn't be laughing at Stram," Wat said. "He's a good dog and brave and everything. Isn't he, Miss Ainsy?"

Ainsy squeezed his arm. "Of course he is, Wat." She shot Fion a warning look that had all the spontaneity of warmed-over cabbage. "They don't mean Stram any harm. It's all in fun, pay them no mind."

Somewhat mollified, Wat dug into his second helping while the conversation turned to other topics. Watching him, Kern could only smile. He was big and simple-minded, and his good nature shone in his broad features like the sun coming through a break in a cloud overhang. Kern had taken an instant liking to him, and he to Kern. He'd come to the room where Kern lay bored, late in the afternoon, shy and awkward at first, sitting on the edge of the bed as though it were made of the finest bone china. Kern had thanked him for his part in the rescue and that put Wat even more ill at ease.

So, to draw him out of his shyness, Kern regaled him with stories of his travels—useful things, tales were turning out to be—until they felt like old friends. As he got to know the big man with the boy's face, he came to doubt that there could ever be one unkind thought in the whole of that large body. Providing that Ainsy would let him out of bed, he promised to visit with each and every one of Wat's wards on the following day.

He was introduced to Tolly for the first time—and more properly to Fion—at the supper table. They seemed cast from the same mold, these two, the boy a younger replica of the woman. They had a joke ready for everyone, on any occasion, though their barbs were sharper for each other. Wat received only a gentle teasing. Ainsy, being employer as well as friend, was somewhat deferred to. And Kern, as the newcomer, was treated more as they might a paying guest—with easy banter.

He liked them both, though Fion made him feel the more at home. In a sense, she was archetypal. Did every inn have an easygoing barmaid like her, or did it only seem that way? Her smiles were impulsive, quick, and open. Her jests and comments hinted at a promiscuity that he was sure was more affected than real. Her attire was worn with similar effect and reflected her personality in an unaffected fashion. The result was that she seemed artlessly charming without appearing to invite more than good-natured banter in return for her own. It was a delicate balance she struck, but she kept to it without apparent effort.

Alongside her, Ainsy appeared quite tempered. Physically she was more compact, compared to the darker woman's fuller figure. But it was more than that. Although she was neither as flamboyant nor as garrulous, her presence—at least to Kern—was still the more keenly felt. And, without demeaning Fion, there was a deep quality about Ainsy's reserve that was as secret and mysterious as moonlight in midsummer while it promised something far more enduring than one night's tryst. There was merriment in it—contained, true, but present nevertheless—and strength. It was as though she nurtured some fair blossom that would wilt under the weight of too much exposure, yet would outlast the oldest longstone.

Kern smiled to himself. He was waxing poetic—a dangerous sign. But, though he was an outsider, he was still made to feel a part of the familial sense that lay about the table as though it were as tangible.

And it was this, as much as his attraction for Ainsy, that

worried him. For were it to grow much stronger, were he to attempt to stay. . . . He glanced at Ainsy, then away. Yet whether he looked at her or not, he was haunted by her presence. His nerves were as tightly wound as a young cub on the scent of its first hare. He knew he was making too much of it all. He need only get up and walk out of the door and it would be over. But whether it was a weakness brought on by his wounds, or that self-pity over his loneliness had grown too strong, there was something present this time that could not be overlooked or simply put aside.

It was fear that held him back. He knew its touch all too well. Tera's face floated in his mind. His mother's. His father's. They were strange faces now, belonging to strangers. Bright silver had severed whatever relationship they might have had to him. Bright silver and their fear, their hatred for what he was. To see that look on Ainsy's face . . . on any of their faces. Could he bear it again? Wasn't it better to simply fade from their lives before it went too far? Before the closeness he only vaguely felt became all too real?

He looked at Ainsy again. She was somewhat subdued this evening—at least compared to how she'd been when they were alone earlier today. He wasn't sure if that was due to the presence of the others, or to what she'd seen when she'd changed his bandages this afternoon. She'd been shocked to see the wounds as healed as they were. When he'd protested that they couldn't have been as bad as she'd thought them to be, she only shook her head. Saying she needed to get supper ready, she'd left soon after, unwilling to meet his gaze. Remembering, Kern felt the wrench inside once more. And if she discovered what he truly was?

The man in him worried and feared, weighed misgivings against benefits, pain against joy, the sorrow that might be born against his present loneliness. Like many men, he wore assurance like an armor, while inside he was everything but certain. And while he vacillated between uncertainties, tried to plan ahead when he should have let come what would come for once, the wolf side of his nature spurned such doubts. For though they were one, wolf and man—and the wolf knew loneliness too, for pack life was withheld from him—yet in many ways the wolf was the stronger. Unlike the man he could live day to day, reap the rich harvest when it was there for the reaping, and give little thought to it when it was not.

Listening to the wolf, Kern understood. It was he who'd given personalities to the dissimilar parts of his nature. As some people might talk to themselves, so had the man and wolf within, conversing together in the wilds when there was nothing but the stars above and the forest around to commune with. It kept loneliness at bay.

So now he shook the introspective mood from him and tried to relax.

"Just one night," Tolly was saying.

"If the garden's all readied and there are no guests," Ainsy replied.

"There's to be a fiddler, you know."

"And many's the lusty farm lad," Fion said, giving Kern a teasing glance. "You should think of coming yourself, Ainsy."

"And who'll look after the inn while we're gallivanting about?"

Fion grinned. "We'll put up a big sign: 'Help yourself. Proprietor and staff off on mad jaunt.'"

Ainsy shook her head. She was thinking more of Tomtim than the inn. They could expect few, if any, guests at this time of year.

"I don't think so. But you lot can go. You can take Wat as well, only keep him out of the ale. And any damages—you can pay them out of your own wages."

Tolly saluted. "Aye, aye, Cap'n."

Ainsy smiled and glanced at Kern. "Last year he was to be a miner in Glenhaven—but only until he learned that it's coal and iron they mine there, not jewels and gold. Then this summer we had a sailor staying for a fortnight. . . ." Her shoulders lifted and fell.

"It'll be neither of those two," Tolly replied with mock seriousness. "I'll be an innkeeper, like our good Miss Ainsy, or nothing at all!"

Fion turned to Kern after the general laughter subsided.

"And what of you, Master Kindregan. Will you come to party in the Hay with us, or mope around the inn with our good mistress here?"

Kern glanced at Ainsy. "I think I'd prefer to mope around."

"Don't blame you a bit," Fion said with a wink. "If I were a man—"

"All the farm lads'd be gravely disappointed!" Tolly cried.

Ainsy felt her cheeks redden, but meeting Kern's gaze, she smiled.

Fourth...

Kern spent the following day exploring the area around the Tinker. The inn proper and its outbuildings were scattered over a quarter acre, with the trees of the Tamwood two miles back from the rear of the inn. Between the wood and the buildings were an orchard, the gardens, and beehives, each kept neat and in its place with orderly hedges of hawthorn and gooseberry and stone fences. The latter were made from fieldstone and barely a foot high.

South were the peaks of the Winders Mountains and the road that cut through Winders Pass. It crossed the Penwater in front of the inn and headed north to Hay-on-Pen. Before introducing him to the livestock under his care, Wat took Kern down to the bridge and showed him where he'd been found. The bootprints were still visible, but whatever scent there had been, was long since gone. Casting back and forth along the riverbank, nostrils widening, Kern caught only the vaguest trace of some elusive and unfamiliar scent.

"You think they were kimeyn?" he asked.

Wat nodded gravely. He put his own big foot alongside the bootprints. "What else could they have been, Master Kern?"

Kern shrugged. He'd given up trying to get Wat to drop the "master" yesterday afternoon. As far as Wat was concerned, everyone had a "miss" or "master" tacked onto the front of their name, depending on their sex.

Clambering up the bank, Kern filed the scent away in his memory. Whatever had left it was something he had no knowledge of. It could well be kimeyn, for all he knew. There were stranger things than they abroad. Shapechangers and . . . harpers. His lips tightened as he thought of the harper in his hunting blacks. Sharp anger flooded him and he wondered that he'd let the harper slip from the forefront of his thoughts. Where was he now? Did he think his quarry slain in the river, as well he should be, or was the hunt still on?

His own wolf scent gave him no trouble with the livestock. He charmed them to accept him, glittering eyes hypnotizing, dulling their fears. But it was as much the fact that he meant them no harm and they sensed it, as anything else. There were times in the forest when a stag could drink beside a well-fed wolf and know itself safe. Another time they might play the ancient game of hunter and hunted, but for that one moment they shared an understanding.

So it was in the inn yard. The goats, the pigs, and donkey were perhaps too domesticated even to see him as a threat. The chickens reacted with deep-rooted instinct, but the charm soothed them. The barn cat ignored him. Only Stram was different.

The dog was too close a cousin to be taken in by the wolf charm. The hackles rose on his neck when Kern drew near him and he growled deep in his throat. And no matter how Wat coaxed him, he wouldn't allow himself to be petted, little say approached.

"He's a good dog," Wat said mournfully. "And always friendly."

"Don't worry about it," Kern replied.

He saw Ainsy watching them from the kitchen window and wished she hadn't seen it. Unreasonably, he connected the dog's acceptance to hers. For didn't dogs sense the true worth of a man? He shook his head, irritated with the thought. But as the dog's growls continued, he felt his own neck hairs rise and had the sudden urge to meet Stram's challenge. And wouldn't that be a sight, the two of them at each other's throats, rolling about on the packed dirt of the inn yard? Kern smiled mirthlessly and walked off.

But that night, when all were abed, he stole from his room and out into the night. He removed his bandages, along with his clothes, and took his wolfshape to stalk the inn yard. Though his wounds were healing well, he still limped in his wolfshape. His keen nostrils soon found Stram asleep by the front of the barn door and he moved downwind.

He padded stiff-legged and silent as a cloud's shadow across the yard. Before Stram was even aware of his presence, he was standing over him, jaws near the hound's throat. He rumbled a low warning, deep in his chest, and Stram awoke, started to move, then lay still, eyes rolling. Slowly Kern backed away. He stood erect and still, his tail horizontally in line with his spine as he stared at the dog. His gaze was unblinking and as sharp as a razor's stropped edge.

For long moments they faced each other. Who knows what thoughts flickered in the dog's mind as he measured the threat of his wild cousin? But at length he rolled over, moving as slowly as Kern had backed away. With his belly lowered and his tail held down, he turned slightly away from the wolf, his ears laid back and the corners of his mouth drawn back in a submissive grin.

His gaze never leaving the dog's, Kern nodded slightly. He took his manshape again and reached out his hand, laying it on top of the dog's trembling head.

"Do we have an understanding, then?" he asked. His voice was so low that it carried no more than a yard. His lips drew back in a feral grin. "We are kin, you and I, though the one's tamed and the other only half so. Give credence to my play at being the man and we need never meet in combat. What say you to that?"

He stroked the dog under the ear, ruffling the soft hairs there. Gradually, Stram's trembling eased.

"So. You understand, do you? Shall we seal our bargain as our wild kin do?"

He took his wolfshape once more and they set off across the inn yard, crossing the fields, running under the bare limbs of the apple trees in the orchard. For all his three-legged gait, Kern set a swift pace. Soon they were running in the forest, hound and wolf, the night and the trees forging a bond between them. The bond was sealed when Kern brought down a hare and, turning his bloodied jaws to the dog, offered the kill to him. Nervously, Stram edged forward, the blood filling his nostrils with a wild scent that echoed in the thunder of his pulse. Kern nudged him with his muzzle and the dog hesitated no longer. Then, side by side, they fed.

In the morning, when Kern stepped into the inn yard, Stram came bounding across it to nuzzle his hand. He smiled at Wat's bewilderment and saw that Ainsy, too, was watching.

"Hard to tell a dog's moods sometimes, isn't it?" he remarked.

That day he worked with the others in the garden, studiously ignoring Ainsy's protests. The run last night had done him a world of good. And though his arm was still stiff, it was usable. He put in a half day's work, then, not wanting to put undue strain upon the shoulder, lazed the rest of the afternoon. That evening after supper, he walked in the orchard with Ainsy, smiling at an inner comparison between the peaceful image they made now and the wolf and the hound that had loped under these same boughs yester eve.

Tonight the sky was clear. The moon was the pale cream of the tallow candle in his room. They walked side by side, not touching, but Ainsy's scent filled his nostrils with the heady perfume that was uniquely hers and, close as she was, he could almost feel her body heat like fire on his skin. The night held its breath around them, pausing when they paused, sighing when they moved on. Underlying the pulse of their heartbeats, the soft footfall of their passage, the rustle of the dried apple leaves underfoot, the wind's murmur in the boughs above, the intake and exhaling of their breathing, all took on musical cadences and built up into a melody. When they trembled, it was not with the night's chill.

Stopping at the far borders of the orchard, they looked back the way they'd come, Ainsy leaning against the rickety stile there, Kern idly plucking at the twigs of the autumn-bare hawthorns that made up the hedge. The lights of the inn twinkled merrily through the apple trees, clearly visible now where in summer the laden boughs would enwrap the orchard into its own private world.

Within those stone walls were friends, Kern realized, did he only take the chance. And beside him . . . Ainsy had won his affection without effort, simply by being who she was. She had his feelings skittering inside him as no woman had before. The moment was magical and he knew then, with absolute clarity, that she could have his heart for the taking, that it was hers already. It needed but the one touch to bind him to her, time without end.

As though she read his mind, Ainsy slipped her hand into the crook of his arm. Through the cloth of his sleeve, the touch of her hand was like a static spark. Her head was tilted back, only slightly for he was not much taller than she was, and the moonlight transformed her face into such a vision of loveliness that he could no more resist than a child might a sweetstick.

Tentatively, he lowered his lips to hers. As they parted under his and the kiss grew more involved, it was only with a great effort that Kern drew back. This was not the time. This was too soon. A little short of breath, they faced each other. Ainsy wore her hair loose this eve and it had spilled across her cheek. Kern brushed it aside and she pressed her cheek against his hand.

"Who are you?" she whispered.

Unspoken, but understood, were other questions. Why do you move me as you do? Can I trust you not to hurt me? Questions lovers had asked each other since time immemorial. Questions for which there were no pat answers.

Kern said nothing. He leaned forward and kissed her again, lightly this time. The taste of her skin was sweet on his lips. Then taking her hand in his, he led her back to the inn. At the door he paused and turned to her, the moon highlighting his face.

"I would never see you hurt," he said. "That's all I can promise you."

"I can't ask for more," she said, and slipped into his arms for a last kiss before they rejoined the others.

With Kern's help, they finished readying the garden for winter the following afternoon. The dark earth was turned with spades and the pig manure spread over every square inch of it. When the last of the dung was laid down and compost bunched around the cut-back stems of the perennials, Tolly let loose with a whoop and flung his rake in the air.

"Done at last!" He turned to Fion. "Want to wrestle to see who gets the first bath?"

Fion smoothed down her dress. "What? And take the chance of breaking an arm? What'll I hold the lads with, then?"

"There's water enough for you both," Ainsy said. "And see that Wat gets cleaned up as well!" she called after them.

That afternoon had seen two travelers pass the inn—a merchant with a late load of goods bound for Bridgeford, and a monk of the Uruth faith, planning to winter in Toome if he could make it through the Yern Pass at the far end of the valley before it was snowed in for the winter. The merchant stopped long enough for an ale, the monk for tea. Ainsy asked after her uncle, but neither had news.

Seeing the worry grow stronger in her eyes, Kern understood why she wasn't joining the others for the party in Hay-on-Pen. He wished again that there was something he could do to alleviate her fears, but knew she could only wait. The Kingdom of Thurin, of which Penenghay Valley was only a small corner, was broad and wide. To go searching for one tinker and his wagon. . . . Kern sighed. He rubbed his hands together and looked toward the river.

"Well, I'm for a washup as well."

"What? In the river?"

"Where else? The baths are all taken."

Ainsy shook her head. "Well, at least you're consistent. But the water's freezing, and if you knock your head again, Arn knows where you'll end up this time. Surely you can wait a half hour or so?"

Kern agreed readily enough. He didn't like to propagate a lie, especially with her, especially now, but it had come more important than ever to hide the wolf from her and the others. If a plunge in icy water helped . . . Better that than having to explain the harper and his feragh, and what exactly they'd been hunting that was red-furred and wild.

An hour and a half later, Tolly had the donkey hitched to the cart and was perched on the driver's seat. Fion joined him, with a poke in the ribs and a cry for room, and Wat stood nearby. It was a three-hour trip to the Foxfire Inn, where the party was to be, and they'd take turns riding and walking.

Before they were off, Fion took Kern aside.

"Be gentle with her, Kern Kindregan, or whatever your name is." Cutting off his protest, she went on. "No. It doesn't matter. But I'll tell you this. I've three great strapping brothers at home and they're all older. But no sister, for all that I've always wanted one. Ainsy . . . she's become the younger sister I never had. And the lads here are like my brothers. We're a family here at the Tinker, missing only Tomtim. You can be a part of it, and we'll welcome you. But don't play us false. I know you're hiding something and I don't care what it is. Just be true to us, here and now, and we'll be true to you. Agreed?"

Kern nodded, a little taken aback at her intensity. Fion grinned suddenly.

"Well?" she demanded, tapping him on the nose with her finger. "Aren't you going to wish us a good time?"

"Oh, aye." He had to laugh.

"Take care, Kern."

He and Ainsy waved them off, watching the wagon bounce along the rutted road, the laughter of the three of them trailing along behind.

"What did Fion have to say?" Ainsy asked. "She seemed so serious."

"She was giving me fair warning."

"Of what?"

"Of what to do in case of a sudden onslaught of guests."

Ainsy laughed, but then an awkward silence fell between them. They were alone, she realized. Herself and a strange man who moved her in ways other men never had. They were both adults, but at this moment seemed more like two shy children first meeting each other. She looked at him and wondered what he was thinking. She remembered the unanswered riddles that added to his strangeness; the look about him that first morning as he crouched like some animal against the wall; Stram's odd behavior, one day grim and the next fawning over him. There were mysteries afoot here for which she had no answers.

But then she recalled yester eve and the walk in the orchard, his touch gentle on her cheek and the taste of his lips; the easy camaraderie as he worked side by side with them, turning the garden and laying the manure. Everyone had their mysteries, she supposed. It was only her liking for him that made her so keen to unriddle his. And though that liking, which was growing oh so quickly into something deeper, alarmed her with its suddenness as much as it gladdened her, she realized that it was the novelty of the situation that had her in such a tizzy. Could Fion read her thoughts, she'd be laughing. But hadn't Fion experienced this same sense of dislocation the first time she'd been with a man? Knowing her, probably not.

Ainsy sighed. What was drumming in her heart was not something that could be dealt with in a sober manner. Emotions were never easy to define, be they anger, sorrow, or whatever it was that she felt just now.

"It's nearing suppertime," she said at last, trying to set the jumble of perplexing thoughts aside. Don't try to rationalize it all, she told herself. Remember Fion's advice. Go with the moment. Well, the moment was at hand. "Want to give me a hand?"

"I peel a mean 'tater," Kern said.

"How are you at trimming greens?"

Kern grinned. "Skilled beyond measure."

"Well, come on then and we'll put those skills to the test."

Whatever the evening might have held for them was changed by a knock on the door. They'd finished a supper of beans, corn, and roasted ham, and were sitting in a nook of the common room, chairs pulled close to the merry fire that crackled in the small hearth, mugs of mulled wine warming their hands.

"Who could that be?" Ainsy said.

"This is still an inn, isn't it?"

Ainsy pulled a face at him and went to see who it was.

Kern trailed along behind her. He was both relieved and disappointed at the interruption. They'd shared an easy closeness at supper and before the fire. But underlying it was the implication that they would share more than simple conversation tonight. What it would be or how it would begin was uncertain. But it lay there between them and they were both eager and nervous about it. Neither had the polished charm of a courtier, or the experience. So they approached it gradually, conscious of each other's hesitations, unhurried more from shyness than a lack of desire.

"I thought everybody'd be at the Foxfire," Ainsy said as she undid the door's bolt.

"Unless it's your uncle."

Worry creased her brow as she thought of Tomtim. "No. He'd never knock. He'd just come in through the kitchen door. We don't keep it locked. Well, here's your chance to put Fion's advice to use."

The door opened on a stranger, burly and dark-bearded, wrapped in a bulky cloak.

"Good even' to you both," he said. "I feared you were locked shut and I'd have to trek all the way down to Hay-on-Pen. Brrr. There's a nip in the air, I don't mind saying."

They stepped aside to let him enter.

"What's the chance of a bite of something? I'm not proud. So long as it's filling and I can wash it down with a warm cuppa."

"Cold roast's all we have, if you don't mind setting to in the kitchen."

"Kitchen's always the warmest place," the stranger said.

Kern took the man's cloak and hung it by the door. The stranger set his pack under it and blew on his hands, rubbing them together.

"It'll snow soon, I'm thinking. The name's Orsden, but folks just call me Gaffer."

"I'm Ainsy Tennen." She introduced herself with a curtsy. "And this is Kern. Will you be wanting a room?"

"A room? I should think so. Damned if I'll walk another step tonight. What I need is a smaller pack. Or stronger shoulders. Getting old, is what it is. Not too busy tonight, are you?" he added as they walked through the common room.

"There's a party down at the Foxfire tonight. Do you know it?"

"Aye. Know it well. All the better I didn't push on. I'm no' in the mood for partying tonight."

He plunked himself down at the kitchen table and stretched out his legs with a sigh.

"I keep forgetting this damn mountain weather," he complained. "The days're fine enough and all, but the nights! Bah!"

"Wine or tea?" Ainsy asked.

"Whichever's on. So long's it's hot."

While she poured him a mug of mulled wine, Kern cut slabs from the roast. He brought a heaping plate with a half loaf of bread on the side. Gaffer took a long swig of the wine, then set it down with a grin.

"Bridgeford grapes," he said. "There's no better. But the spices're your own?"

Ainsy nodded. "What's the news from beyond?" she asked as he tore off a chunk of bread.

"This 'n' that. No' much new. Tigshire's got itself a new

lord. The old one went and fell off his horse while ahunting and broke his fool neck."

Through a mouthful of bread and roast ham, he related what news there was. When Ainsy asked her usual question after her uncle, Gaffer frowned.

"Funny you should ask," he said. "I saw a wagon just like you've described in the pass this afternoon. It was late, getting on dark, when I saw it sitting a ways off the road under some pines. I gave it a hail, but there was no answer and I didn't have the time to go have a look-see. A strange place to be camping, I thought, there being no water near, but. . . ." He shrugged. "Tinkers. Who knows why they do anything? Is it someone you know?"

"My uncle."

Gaffer nodded. "Aye. 'The Yellow Tinker.' I shoulda thought of that myself. Well, he's camped in the pass, Mistress Tennen, so I'm sure he'll be down come the morning."

Ainsy's face had grown drawn and pale as he spoke. "That close to home," she said. "He wouldn't have camped unless something's happened to him. . . ."

Gaffer shook his head. "Now you don't know that. The road's been as quiet as a pundar asleeping under a hedge when he should be chasing after his lord's cattle. There's been no word of brigands for a month or better. Maybe your uncle's just gotten himself drunk and didn't care to try the grade with the dark coming on."

"He wouldn't do that." She turned to Kern, hand at her mouth, eyes wide. "Oh, Kern. What if something's happened to him?"

"He's as safe there as in his own bed," Gaffer said. "What could harm him? Old Duorn hung the last brigand on that road a week before he took that fall from his horse. There's been nary a word of trouble since."

But Kern was thinking of a harper, dressed in hunting blacks, and the great silvery beast that his music gave life to. The wolf stirred in him. His eyes narrowed to slits. Safe? How could there be safety with someone like that abroad? A low growl started in his chest, but he stilled it before it was audible.

"I'll go look for him," he said, rising from the table.

"Kern! You're still recovering yourself and it's dark. I won't allow it! You don't even know the way."

"The way's easy enough. I just follow the road."

"But . . ."

"You're worried," he said. "And have been for days. Well, I'll worry for you." She'd left the table herself and he gripped her shoulder, fitting what he hoped was a reassuring smile to his lips. "I won't be long. How far did you say it was, Gaffer?"

"A goodly way. Took me three hours—but that was downhill. It's foolish to go out there. Besides, a tinker knows how to take care of himself when he's on the road. He'll be all right."

Kern heard the ringing of a harp in his ears. "And if he's not?"

Gaffer shrugged. "Do as you want. I'm no' the one to stop you."

"Kern. . . ."

He shook his head. "Don't fret about it. If he's there, I'll have him back to you before morning."

And if he's not? he asked himself. He tried not to think of the feragh's silvery fur, gleaming in the moonlight, and the sharp discordance of the harper's music.

"Then take a weapon at least. There's a sword hanging over the mantel."

"I wouldn't know how to use it."

Already he could feel the road under his wolf paws. What need did he have of weapons? Against the feragh? another part of him asked. Did you fare so well the first time? Kern shook his head, stilling the inner tumult.

At the door Ainsy took hold of his arm. "Be careful," she said, her upturned face knit with worry.

"I will."

The earlier shyness of the evening dissolved at that moment. He took her in his arms and she clung to him, trembling. When he left, it was with the taste of her lips on his and her cry of "Luck!" ringing in his ears.

Once out of sight of the inn, he stopped and stripped his borrowed clothes from him, rolling them in a bundle that he fastened against his neck so that it hung around his chest. Trembling a little from the night's chill, he willed the change to come to him. A moment he stood, neither man nor beast but some terrible hybrid of the two, upright but furred, with a wolf's jaw but a man's brow, then he was loping along the road, powerful muscles propelling him at a mile-eating gait. His shoulder felt strong, but he still favored the one leg somewhat. It would be a long run.

Ainsy stood in the doorway until he disappeared into the swell of darker shadows beyond the perimeter of the inn's lights. She never saw the change, nor the wolf that he became. In her mind she pictured the man she knew, trudging along the road in the dark. Slowly she closed the door and made her way back to the kitchen. Gaffer bid her a good even' and made for his room, leaving her to wait on her own, with nothing but the fire's flames to keep her company.

Fion and Tolly came rolling in a few hours before dawn, with many a hushed laugh and giggle. They'd deposited Wat in the barn, put up the donkey, and were making their way to their own rooms when they saw the light in the kitchen.

"Ah, Ainsy!" Fion cried. She was more than a little tipsy, so she never gave a thought as to why Ainsy was still up and sitting alone in the kitchen. "Such a night! You should have come. There was—"

"A harper!" Tolly broke in excitedly. "A real bard!"

"He played music on his harp the like I've never heard before."

"And the tales he told!"

They told the story as though they were one, each taking a turn with no discernible break between who said one sentence and who the next.

"He said he saw a wolf—right here in the valley!"

"Old Camm told him he was mad. For you know there haven't been wolves here for a hundred years or better."

"But the harper told him no. Saw one, he said, and where there's one—"

"There's many. . . ."

Their voices trailed off.

"Where's Kern?" Fion asked, her voice gone soft. "Oh, Ainsy. What's happened?"

She saw now, from the red eyes, that Ainsy'd been crying. And—Arn above!—it must be nearly sunrise. What was she still doing up at this hour? Kern. . . . An abrupt anger started in her. What had he done to her?

"He's gone," Ainsy said. "He went looking for Tomtim. Gaffer—he showed up this evening. He told us he'd seen the wagon in the pass, so Kern went looking for him. But he's been gone for hours."

Gaffer? Kern looking for Tomtim?

"Tell it to us from the beginning," Fion said, suddenly sober.

They got the tale from her, bit by bit.

"Can't leave you alone for a minute, can we?" Fion said, trying to lighten Ainsy's mood.

"Fion, please. . . ."

The darker-haired woman nodded. "I'm sorry. But think a moment, Ainsy. It'd take him the whole night to get up into the pass and back down again."

"I know. That's what I keep telling myself. But I just feel that something terrible's happened. Why would the wagon even be there, Fion?"

"I don't know." She glanced at Tolly, then back. "We put Wat to bed before we came in. If you like, we could wake him and all go have a look for them."

Ainsy shook her head. " No. I know I'm just being stupid. We just have . . . to wait. But it's not easy."

"It never is," Fion replied.

Ainsy rubbed her eyes with the sleeve of her dress.

"Tell me about the party," she said. "It'll take my mind off my worries. You said there was a harper?"

"The like of which you've never seen," Tolly said. "You'd swear he was a wizard for the sounds he could pull from his strings. His name's Tuiloch and he means to winter in the valley. . . ."

Fifth...

The moon was down and the night grew darker still as an overhang of clouds drifted in from the north, shrouding the stars. A little more than three hours had passed since Kern left the Inn of the Yellow Tinker behind. Given that he still favored his left somewhat, and that the road through the rough terrain was both tortuous and steep, he should now be nearing the place Gaffer had described.

His breath wreathed about his muzzle, but the cold could not penetrate his winter growth of dense underfur. In high winter he could sleep in the open, his muzzle and nose between his rear legs and bushy tail covering his face. In the most bitter cold, he could reduce the flow of blood near his skin to conserve even more heat. On a night like this, he didn't even feel the cold.

The wind was at his back once more, scudding the clouds above and driving his own scent ahead of him. So he relied on hearing mostly, his ears cocked as he loped to catch even the most minuscule sound, and on his eyesight, which was never keen in wolfshape. And with the night this dark. . . .

Topping a rise where the granite and sandstone cliffs leaned over the road but opened into a wooded dale ahead, he saw the fire. It leaped and danced in the darkness, throwing strange shadows through the pines, tongues of yellow and red flame garish and bright. This was no campfire. More a blaze. A bonfire. The wagon!

Kern faded along the cliffside, scouting the lay of the land ahead. A new surge of adrenaline pulsed through his wolfish veins. The cliff blocked the wind from behind him, but told him nothing of what lay ahead. He heard the crackle and roar of the fire as he worked his way closer, padding under the pines. His neck hairs hackled when he saw the shapes of men silhouetted against the flames. Three. No, four. Closer still and he could make out their voices.

Concealed in a stand of young trees, he took manshape again. As a wolf, his lupine senses sometimes fed too much data for him to concentrate overly much on mannish affairs. It was always easier to assimilate a situation and make decisions without the wolf thoughts clouding his judgment. Just as the wolf was superior in certain situations—tracking, hunting, simple survival in the wilds—so too was the man. It was often too easy to distract the wolf. It needed only a scent, or a feeling too subtle for man senses, to make it skittish. As well, the wolf's ire, once roused, was hard to quell.

Naked, Kern felt the night's chill, but didn't take the time to dress. It would only hamper him if action was needed. He crept forward some more, to take further stock of the situation. The carpet of pine needles made a crisscrossing pattern on his knees. His nostrils flared as he sought the feragh's scent, listened for the harper's hated music. But all he heard were gruff voices raised in argument. And as he drew closer still, the wood smoke covered all odors.

"—tinker trash," one of the men was saying.

His face was turned from the fire and swallowed by darkness. The dancing firelight made it difficult to make out any of their features. The shadows created strange highlights. Even had Kern known them, he wasn't sure that he'd have recognized them. But scent, for all the wood smoke, and sight and sound told him what he wanted to know. Neither harper nor feragh was present. These were only plain brigands. They wore homespun trousers and shirts, leather boots and vests. One had a sheepskin jacket with the wool side turned out.

"I saw t' gold," another muttered. "A fistful of shiny gold coins."

"Aye," the first said.

Kern edged closer, trying to catch a view of Ainsy's uncle. With luck, while the thieves were bickering, he might be able to slip in and out with the old man before they were the wiser. He had no desire to fight the four of them, nor test the edges of their blades. And if one of them had a silver dagger at his belt, spoils stolen from some merchant? One blow from a weapon like that and his body would not heal so swiftly.

Then he saw Tomtim and his hopes sank. The brigands had tied him up near the fire and stripped him. As he watched, one of the men caught the tinker by the hair and dragged his face close to the flames.

"Time to speak," the man who held him said. "Spill t' tale, or we'll fry you, bit by bit. We know you had t' coin, old man. Where's it hid?"

Kern stifled a growl. In the firelight he could see the ugly bruises on Tomtim's face and chest. When the tinker gave no answer and the brigand struck him across the face, adding another bruise on the already darkened cheek, Kern knew he could not wait. Yet what to do? In manshape he'd be no match for the four of them, and even the wolf would be hard-pressed. He had surprise on his side, but little else. And if they had silver . . .

Another of the men drew a branch from the fire. He swung it in the air so that the end of it gleamed bright red. Then, with two of them holding Tomtim down, he brought it near the tinker's face.

"Gentle it is we've been so far," he said. "You've lost t' wagon and lie bare-assed and helpless. P'rhaps you can stand t' loss of some pride, but an eye? Or t' both of them?"

"I told you," Tomtim said. It was plain from his voice that he knew they'd believe him no more now than they had before. "I was paying a debt in Cleston. Whatever else I had, you have now."

"Five coins? You think we'll settle for five when there's a sack to be had?"

He brought the firebrand closer to Tomtim's face, singeing the old man's brows.

"You've buried it," he said. "Somewheres 'tween here and Cleston. Tell us where and we'll set you free."

Kern trembled with anger. Sweet stars above! It was men just as these that spoke of his shapechanging with repugnance. Yet see what they would do to satisfy their greed. He could wait no more. Manshape might not do on its own, nor the wolf either, but some hybrid of the two? Something to cut the courage from them and raise such a superstitious dread that they'd not stop to think, little say fight?

He rose to his feet and willed the change, stopping it partway. Red fur covered his body, but he remained upright. His neck sank low against his chest. His face lengthened, mannish teeth becoming wolfish fangs. His legs were bowed somewhat, but the thrust of a half-grown tail from his posterior balanced him. He rumbled a threatening growl low in his chest and loosed it through lips that were neither man's nor beast's. The sound rose up from his diaphragm, low and resonating, inhuman.

The brigands froze. The first turned, saw Kern's charge, and recoiled. He stepped back, treading on one of his fellows, his features gone liquid, eyes rolling. He tore at his belt, trying to draw his sword from its battered sheath, but Kern was upon him. A blow from a limb that was something between arm and forepaw, sent the man staggering into the fire. His hair and clothing blazed. He flung himself free of the flames, screaming and rolling in the grass.

The two that were holding Tomtim bolted. Only the man with the firebrand stood his ground. He swung his makeshift weapon, low and sudden. Sparks shattered the night air when it connected with Kern. As he lifted his arm to strike again, Kern shook off the effects of the first blow and leaped at him. He changed shape in midair and tore out the man's throat with a wolf's jaws. The brigand was dead as he hit the ground.

Kern straddled his victim. The man's blood was like fire in his mouth. It set his brain spinning. He saw his first opponent struggling to escape and closed the distance between them in three bounds. The man ran. With the taste of blood still firing him, Kern hamstrung him, finishing him off as he tumbled to the sod. The acrid stench of burned flesh and hair mingled with the scent of fresh blood, but neither could still the sensations that coursed through lupine nerves. Kern lifted his head and howled. He shook his muzzle back and forth, casting for the scent of the two that had escaped.

Then, like a pinprick of light awakening in a sea of darkness, the man in him realized what he had done.

Slain men. Tasted their blood. He'd meant only to chase them off. He'd never meant to kill. He. . . .

The wolfshape fell from him and he tumbled to the ground, pressing his face against the grass. He had never slain a man before. Not in wolfshape. Only once as a man, and that had been more an accident than a planned deed. The man had jumped him out back of an inn and when Kern threw him off of his shoulder, he'd cracked his head on a stone and died. But this. . . . Old fears reared in him. Werewolf. Nightstalker. The damned who rubbed shoulder to shoulder with his fellows by day and fed on their flesh by night.

He tasted the blood still on his lips, in his mouth, trickling hot down his throat, and retched. Again and again he heaved, until his stomach was empty and the sour taste of bile had all but covered that of the sweet-salty blood. Weakly he raised himself on his hands and knees. His naked body felt none of the night's chill, for the cold in his soul was icier still.

He was no different, he tried to tell himself. He'd attacked with just cause and they—the ones that were dead—had deserved to die. It was not as though he'd stalked them senselessly, slaying as the legends would have it. Had he not done what he had, Tomtim would be dead, and Ainsy without her uncle. Ainsy. . . . How could he face her? Again the pungent taste of blood overrode the bile and he dry-heaved until his sides ached. He saw

Tera's face and knew what she'd seen in him, understood the horror and revulsion. He saw his parents and wondered why he'd not simply let them destroy him. It was they who had brought him into the world. Surely they were responsible for seeing to his death? Surely it was the onus laid upon them, that they must dispatch the monster they had given life to?

It was something like a fever that overcame him, filling his head with horrific images, his teeth chattering, limbs trembling. Fever. Shock. Or perhaps just residual weakness from the harper's attack. By the movement of the stars, he realized it had been an hour and no more that he lay there, wallowing in self-hate and fever. But slowly, lifting through the delirium that gripped him, came the strength that had sustained him through all the years. He was what he was, neither better nor worse than other men. Only different. What had happened this night changed nothing. He took up his earlier argument and, calmer now, the fever wearing off, could accept it without recriminations. The brigands had called their fate down upon themselves. Two of them were dead and the other two would probably put a hundred leagues between them and this place before ever they dared to stop their headlong flight. Had he not acted when he did, Tomtim might be blinded, at the least, dead at worst. A lingering shiver sped up his spine. But it was not as much from the horror, this time, as from the cold.

He stood and raised his face to the starred skies. They

remained unchanged, wheeling in their solemn dance despite what dramas were enacted under their pale light. They were sparks of brightness in the wild sea of night. They did not judge him Should he then judge himself? He searched his soul and found that, for better or worse, he had accepted what had happened. He must go on. Below in the valley lay the hope of a new life, friends and a home, the wild woods still to roam. And Ainsy. . . .

It was a stronger man who returned to where he'd left his bundle of clothes. He neither turned his face nor flinched when he saw his handiwork lying bloodied and still in the light of the dying fire. A nerve jumped in his cheek, but that was all. He felt pity. And lingering anger when he knelt down by the still figure of Ainsy's uncle. The tinker stirred under his touch.

"No more," Tomtim moaned. "As Arn is my witness, I've told you the truth."

"It's over now," Kern said.

He wiped the old man's brow with a gentle hand. Taking a knife from the belt of one of the dead brigands who would need it no more, he cut the tinker's bonds. Eyelids fluttered as Kern rubbed Tomtim's wrists, trying to restore circulation. The tinker opened his eyes and stared into Kern's face.

"You . . . You're not. . . ."

Kern shook his head. "I'm here to help you. The others are gone . . . those that live."

"Those that live. . . ." Tomtim nodded weakly. "I

remember. I thought I saw . . . some creature from a nightmare come charging. But it came to help me. It was like a bear, only upright like a man, and had a face like . . . like a wolf. It was you?"

There was no fear in the old man's voice, only curiosity.

"It was I. But I think the firelight played tricks on your eyes. As you can see: I'm as much a man as you are. Haven't even a beard."

"Aye. Aye. Perhaps."

Tomtim's eyes were overly bright, his features drawn and pale against the discoloration of his bruises. But his gaze was piercing and intelligent. Kern knew a sudden return of self-doubt. If the old man saw through his explanation. . . . He didn't want to lie, but he didn't want to lose a chance of a normal life at the Tinker either. But what thoughts Tomtim had, he kept to himself.

"Man or beast," he said. "I thank you. How did you come to be here at my need?"

"I was looking for you. Your niece has been worried, and when a traveler brought word of your wagon sitting here off the road. . . ." Kern shrugged.

"My wagon . . . gone. . . ."

"You've your life," Kern said. "Surely that's worth more?"

"Aye. Perhaps I'm too old to go road wending and this's Arn's way of telling me."

Kern shook his head. "The Moon Lady was never so

harsh. This is ill-chance, nothing more. Though you might remember not to show your gold around. There are some who see that only as a challenge."

While they spoke, Kern gathered up the tinker's clothes and helped him dress. "Rest here a bit longer," he said, "while I see what can be salvaged from this mess."

While Tomtim huddled near the fire, Kern scavenged what he could from the tinker's belongings. He heaped them in a pile beside the fire, adding to it the weapons of the slain brigands and the few items of value he found on their corpses. The bodies themselves he dragged onto the fire. It wouldn't do to have Tomtim, or any other passerby, see the manner of their deaths. He added wood to the coals and the fire leaped up, hiding his handiwork in its yellow-red flames. The stink of burning flesh filled the air, though Kern, with his keener senses, was more aware of it than the tinker. The wind sent the brunt of it off up the pass.

"Can you walk, do you think?" Kern asked.

"I can try. Lend me your shoulder."

Kern helped him to his feet and supported him. Gingerly, the old man tested his strength.

"I'll need help. It's a ways still to the Tinker."

With a brigand's sword, Kern cut Tomtim a staff. He thought suddenly of the horses that had pulled the tinker's wagon, but a quick survey of the campsite showed where they'd been tethered. Hoofprints in the sod and frayed rope hanging from a tree bough were all that remained.

They must have broken free during his attack, the howl of a wolf and its scent lending their muscles the strength needed to break their fetters and escape. With any luck, they would have run down the pass into the valley where the inn folk could catch them.

"I gathered what I could of your belongings," Kern said, indicating the heap by the fire. "We could take some with us and come back for the rest with a cart."

Tomtim made his way to Kern's side and stared at what was left of his wagon. A haunted look filled his eyes and slowly he shook his head. "There's little of any worth left," he said. "My tools, perhaps. We can return for them."

"There are these as well."

Kern dropped five gold coins into the tinker's outstretched hand.

Tomtim stared at them for long moments before he closed his fist and thrust them into a trouser pocket. Then, with Kern's help, he separated what he wished to keep from the ruin of his belongings. Ax heads and knife blades. Metalworking tools. Some pans and pots that had survived the heels of the brigands. A basket of trinkets and knickknacks.

"Little enough to show for my years on the road," Tomtim murmured. "And my wagon. . . ."

He lowered his head, but not before Kern saw the glisten on his eyelashes.

He left the tinker there and, cutting two saplings and

trimming them, began to construct a rude sled. He used strips of charred canvas to carry the load between the shafts. To pull it, he rigged up a shoulder harness from the belts of the dead brigands. When he had the sled loaded, he rejoined the tinker and laid his hand on the old man's shoulder. Dawn was streaking the east, pinking the sky behind the mountain peaks.

"They'll be waiting for us below," he said.

Tomtim started. "What? Oh, aye."

The day began with clear skies, but rapidly grew overcast. In the brighter light, Kern took a closer look at the tinker and wondered anew how he'd survived both the brigands' beating and his years on the road. He was well into his sixties, rope-thin and wiry. His hair was grey and hung to his shoulders, back from the ears to show off the two gold earrings that the brigands hadn't gotten around to taking from him. His cheeks and chin had a day's growth on them, but his mustache was bushy. A survivor, Kern decided, taking in the lined face and the determination still present in the pale blue eyes.

"We'd better be going," he said gently.

Tomtim nodded. "There's nothing left for me here." When he saw the load that Kern had rigged, he shook his head. "There's no need . . ."

Kern shrugged. "I'd rather not have to return."

"Aye. There's that."

There was a strange look in the tinker's eyes as he spoke. Kern wondered what he was thinking of. His own ordeal? The loss of his wagon? Or what he remembered of his rescue? The old man's first words came back to Kern. "Upright like a man, but with a face like a wolf." How much had he seen? How much did he remember?

Kern sighed. He hitched the sled into a more comfortable position, taking care that the leather straps wouldn't rub his old wound. It had stood up to a remarkable amount of abuse through this long night. The strain was beginning to catch up, however, and it had begun to ache now. His whole body felt stiff, for he wasn't fully rested from his own ordeal with the feragh and the river. His lower torso smarted from where the brigand had landed a blow with his firebrand.

Aye, he thought as he set off at an easy pace. They made a fine pair, Tomtim and him. They could both do with a rest.

"Coming?" he called over his shoulder.

Leaning on his staff, Tomtim followed.

Sixth...

A mile or two from the inn, some hours later, they were met by a search party. Except for Fion, who had stayed behind to mind the inn, all were there. Stram leaped about Kern, yapping shrilly. Gratefully, the shapechanger passed the burden of his sled to Wat and rubbed the mongrel's ears. Ainsy ran forward to embrace her uncle, then paused with a stricken look as she took in the blue-black bruises. Before she could say anything, Tomtim drew her close. From the shelter of his arms, she turned to look at Kern. The grateful look in her eyes made the whole of the night worthwhile and strengthened his decision to stay.

"We didn't know what to think," Tolly said. He stood back, holding two shaggy horses by their tattered reins. "When the horses showed up on their own . . ."

"Where is the wagon?" Ainsy asked. "And what happened? I was so worried. And Tomtim. Your face . . ."

"It's a long story," Kern said. "But you can forget about the wagon."

"Forget . . . ?"

"I'll tell you as we walk back."

Tolly gave Tomtim a leg up. The old tinker leaned against his mount's neck, the remnants of his ordeal plain in his haggard features. Mounting behind him, Tolly set off for the inn, leading the other horse. The rest followed at a slower pace.

Kern told the whole tale twice: once on the walk back to the inn, and again sitting around the kitchen for Fion and Tolly. Tomtim was abed now. Outside it had begun to rain, starting with a fine drizzle, but once the wind picked up, the rain battered against the inn's shutters as though demanding entrance. Interspersed with that roar was a staccato of hail.

Watching the storm's tumult through the thick smoky panes of the kitchen window, Kern shivered, appreciating that he was in out of the weather, in manshape, instead of crouching for shelter in the undergrowth of the forest, wearing his wolfshape.

"That there can be men such as that," Fion said, shaking her head.

"How did you best them?" Tolly wanted to know. "You've said nothing about that. There were four of them, and you unarmed. Did you steal a sword and lay at them with it?"

Kern shook his head. "I caught them unawares. The first stumbled into the fire while I grappled with another. The other two, hearing their comrades' screams, must have thought a small army was attacking. It was dark, remember, for all the fire's light. They bolted. I meant only to scare them off, if I could, but . . ." He shrugged uncomfortably. "They left me no choice. I killed two of them. Perhaps they deserved death for what they did to Tomtim and the stars know how many others, but I feel no pride in their deaths."

Tolly was too caught up in his imagination to let it go at that. "But four of them! And you unarmed!"

"Do not make me out the hero, Tolly. There was nothing heroic about the way they died."

"Well, I'm not sorry they're dead," Ainsy said. "And I'd feel safer knowing the other two weren't out there still."

Kern remembered all too well how he himself had felt, seeing the brigands torturing her uncle.

"They won't be back," he said, and tried to keep from his mind the image of wolf jaws snapping at a man's neck and the taste of hot blood. . . . Those other two would remember too. They fled because of fear and that same fear would keep them away.

"They shouldn't have tried to hurt Master Tomtim," Wat said firmly.

Kern looked up, startled. For a moment he thought he'd been thinking aloud, then he saw that Wat had merely taken his time worrying through the problem before making his pronouncement.

"Too true," Kern said, and Wat beamed.

"You're our hero," Tolly said.

"And a modest one too!" Fion added.

Kern forced himself to relax. They knew nothing of the manner of death that had come to the brigands, saw only that one of their own had been threatened and that he had rescued him. It was one more link in the bond that was forming between them and himself. They were not bloodthirsty. They wished only to see justice being done. And, to all intents and purposes, it had been.

The rain had let up somewhat. Tolly rose and added a log to the fire. The wood was still damp and it hissed and crackled as it dried out. Kern finished his tea and tried to suppress a yawn with little success. Ainsy was instantly concerned. It was off to bed for him, then and there, and she'd brook no argument. As Tomtim was occupying his own room, she took him into hers. Kern's tiredness came over him so suddenly that he simply let himself be led to a bed and, tumbled into a deep slumber, giving no thought as to where it was that he lay.

Standing over him, Ainsy sighed good-humoredly. She tugged and pulled at his clothes, dropping them one by one on the floor, and rolled him under the covers.

Kern slept soundly until the middle of the evening. Then his eyes snapped open and his nostrils flared as he sought what had awakened him. It was only Ainsy, setting a candle holder on the nightstand. She sat down on the bed and smiled at him, albeit a little nervously. There was an unreadable something in her eyes that set an echoing emotion thundering through him.

"What time is it?" he asked.

"Late. Time for bed."

Kern nodded a little stupidly, sleep still claiming a part of his mind. Then he looked around, and though he'd never been in her room, he knew where he was. The whole of the room whispered Ainsy, from the vase with its swirling designs and dried flowers, to the pattern of the curtains and the watercolor of a meadow that hung across from the bed. The candlelight flickered and, in the painting, the grasses that the artist had caught with brush and paint seemed to move.

"I've stolen your bed," Kern said, and made to rise.

Ainsy pushed him back against the pillows. "Kern," she said gently. "Don't go—unless you want to."

"I. . . ."

"When you left last night, I . . . I thought perhaps you'd never come back. That something terrible would happen to you. If you'd not killed those brigands, if they'd killed you. . . ." She shivered. "I don't know what I'd've done."

She looked as if she wanted to say more, but couldn't find the words. Instead, she began to unbutton the top of her dress. Kern's gaze was drawn to the movement, then lifted to her face. What had been unreadable in her eyes earlier was so no longer.

She stood and slipped off her dress, leaned forward to blow out the candle. That one vision of her, before the light died in the room, flared in Kern's mind. Then she was in his arms, smooth and warm, her sweet scent filling his nostrils, her unbound hair tumbling about them.

~~~~~

Kern awoke late in the morning. He was alone in the bed, but Ainsy's scent still drifted up to him from the pillows and sheets. Outside the window, the autumn sun was bright. A few hardy sparrows were lifting their voices in a chirping song. Kern stretched and rose with a singing in his own heart. He found his clothes draped over the back of a chair and put them on. Humming to himself, he ran his fingers through his hair and left the room. He met Fion in the hallway.

"Well, good morn to you," she said. Humor bubbled in her eyes.

Kern grinned. "A good morn indeed! Do you know where–"

"Ainsy's in the kitchen."

She left him with a laugh.

He went out through the front door, washed up at the well, then came in through the kitchen. Ainsy glanced up from the hearth where she was frying corn cakes in a flat pan on the hearthstones. She smiled when she saw him, lifting her face for a kiss when he stood by her.

"Last night," she said and blushed a little. "You didn't think I was too bold? I . . . I've never done anything like that before."

"Never too bold," he said, and kissed her again.

Working with Tolly in the barn that afternoon, Kern couldn't help but wonder at his good fortune. To fall in with folk such as these, and to be accepted so readily. . . . He thought of Ainsy and lifted her features in his mind. More than accepted. To be loved.

They were cleaning out stalls for Tomtim's horses. The scent of hay was strong in the air—hay mixed with dung, a homey smell, an honest smell. The pitchfork felt good in Kern's hands as he spread the hay. He thought of the woods and knew that, once in a while, he would still seek out its wonders in wolfshape, but he promised himself, here and now, that he'd wander no more. He had all he needed and could want for nothing more.

"How was the party?" he asked Tolly when they were done.

They were sitting on bales of hay, watching the horses munch their handful of oaks and apple. In all the fluster of yester eve, Kern had never gotten around to asking.

"Grand," Tolly said. "Just grand. I met a girl—ah, such a girl! Her name's Sara and her father works a tract of land just the other side of Hay-on-Pen. I tell you we danced such as I've never danced before. And later, when the harper got up to play and we sat together at a corner table. . . ." His eyes closed as he relived the memory. "There was only the one chair, you see. . . ."

But Kern was no longer listening. At the word *harper,* the warmth of the day froze into a bitter lump in the pit of his stomach. Images of black leather and silver fur flashed through his mind and he heard again the hated music that had driven him to run until he could run no more. Then . . . the cliff's edge . . . the feragh's blow . . . falling and the cold water closing overhead. . . .

"A harper?" he asked, trying to keep his voice level. "What was he like?"

"Like you've never heard before,'" Tolly said. But then he remembered that Kern wasn't from the valley. "Then again, seeing how you've traveled the wide world around, perhaps you have."

Perhaps I have indeed, Kern thought bitterly, though not where you might think I did.

"Still," Tolly went on, "this man was magic itself. He played like *I've* never heard before. He could make you weep or laugh, just with a tug of the strings. His fingers moved like water over them and the sound . . . ah, the sound." He shook his head, the words simply not there to do his description justice.

"He's staying in Hay-on-Pen?"

"At the Foxfire–till the end of the week. But he means to winter in the valley. Tomorrow's his last night near here for a while, for he's off to Bridgeford for a fortnight. We're going back tomorrow night–Fion and I, and perhaps Wat. Sara promised to be there, so I wouldn't miss it for the world. The music and her. . . ." He sighed. "Perhaps Tomtim'll lend me a horse so that I could give her a ride home. Wouldn't *that* be perfect?"

Kern nodded.

"You should come along–you and Ainsy."

"Perhaps we will," Kern said, but his chest was tight with anger and fear.

He should have known that what he'd found here was too good to last. He didn't know why the harper had raised the feragh with his music to hunt him, but the simple fact that he was still here in the valley meant that it would be unsafe for Kern to stay. Yet why should he be driven out? He had as much right as any. . . . Kern shook his head. He'd been about to say *as any man*, but he wasn't a man, was he? He was something else again— part man, aye, but part beast as well. And what were beasts fit for but to hunt? He clenched his fists at his side. He felt so helpless.

"Kern? Are you all right?"

He looked up. Tolly was regarding him worriedly. With an effort, he pushed the turmoil inside him back a little.

"I'm fine," he said. "I was just thinking. Why don't you see what else Ainsy wants us to do? I'll be along in a moment."

Tolly nodded uncertainly. Left to himself, Kern stared at the barn floor. If only he had some defense against the harper's magic. Then he'd face him and be done with it. But there was too much power in the harper. He was not some brigand who could be frightened off by his wolf-shape, and Kern didn't want to make a habit of that anyway. Talk would start up, strangers would be sought out. In any case, the harper could call his own shapes to life with his music. The feragh. Perhaps worse. But to be so helpless. . . . He stood and, picking up the pitchfork, flung it against the wall. It fell with a clatter to the barn floor and lay still.

He regarded the implement dully. Opening and closing his big hands, he wished he had the harper's throat in them. Then slowly he squelched his rage. He didn't have to flee. More than likely, the harper thought him dead. And if the harper remained ignorant, if Kern himself kept out of the mage's way, how could he know that his prey still lived?

The idea of hiding from his foe filled Kern with repugnance, but remembering the power of the harpmagic and the feragh. . . . What else could he do? Against them, his own strength was futile. He was helpless, but damned if he'd run again. He would stay out of the harper's way, but if the time came, no matter that the thought of it filled him with a queasy fear, he would face it. What he'd found here was too precious. He had the choice of fleeing now and knowing the warmth no more, or staying, stealing what days he could, until he and the harper met face-to-face again. And perhaps, just perhaps, that day would never come.

But it wasn't to be as easy as that. When he was with Ainsy later that afternoon, she was bubbling over with excitement over the harper and going to hear him. He couldn't forestall their going—not without having to explain why. He would not lie to her, but he didn't have the courage to tell her the truth. So, barring the arrival of paying guests, they planned to close down the inn and the whole lot of them would make the trip into Hay-on-Pen to hear the harper play.

Seventh...

The Foxfire Inn was smaller than the Tinker, and crowded to the rafters that evening. It sat between a smithy and a carryall shop on Tander's Row, one of two streets that began nowhere, cut across the King's Road through Hay-on-Pen, and emptied into the river. There was a courtyard out back, with a well and three apple trees, and stables where Tolly and Kern put up the horses and cart while the others waited for them out front. Behind the stables were fields, some cultivated, some pasture, and beyond them an arm of the Tamwood.

The inn was half full when they arrived, and filling rapidly. In another hour or so there wouldn't be free room to stand, little say a place to sit. Needles prickled between Kern's shoulder blades as they stepped over the threshold, but he tried to put up as best a face as he could. Having allowed himself to come this far, there was no sense in spoiling it for the others.

There came a general hubbub of greeting at their entrance—for many of the folk knew Fion and Tolly, if not the others—and no quiet way to find a table. Kern wanted to sit in the back, where the light wasn't so strong, but Fion led them to a spot on the edge of the dance floor where tables and benches had simply been pushed aside to open a space, eight feet or so by ten. Room was made for them with a furor of jests and laughter, and there they were: dead across from the hearth where the fiddlers and flute players would stand to play for the dancers and where, later, the harper himself would sit to play.

As surreptitiously as possible, Kern studied the Foxfire's patrons but couldn't see anyone even vaguely resembling the harper. Where was he then? Had he already seen Kern and guessed/ known who he was? The knot remained in Kern's stomach and he wondered again why he was even here. Pride? A need to end it? Or something simpler? He turned to his companions and his heart did its by now familiar flip when he looked at Ainsy.

She sat at his side, decked out in her best dress, radiant with the night's promise of excitement. Her skirt was a deep rust that hugged her waist and hips, then fell down in plaits to just below her knee. The bodice was a rich cream color, with a laced throat and flounced sleeves. Hanging over the back of her chair was a woolen shawl that matched the autumn rust of her dress.

She caught him watching her and leaned over to kiss him soundly on the lips. "Why so grim-faced?" she asked.

He found a smile for her. "Not used to parties, I suppose."

"Neither am I," she replied. "But that's no excuse not to have fun. After all—"

The rest of her words were lost as the music started up. An old fiddler stood at the hearth, pulling quick notes from his instrument, his beard so bushy that Kern was sure he'd catch his bow in it. His leg went up and down, keeping time to the rhythm of the drummer's bodhran. He was a sober-faced man, hunched over his goatskin instrument, the double-headed tipple a blur as he beat away. Completing the trio was a slender woman in her late forties, playing the flute.

The tune they played was a well-known jig called variously "The Rigs of the Tattershall" or "The Tattershall Jig," depending on who the players were. Kern smiled. He'd heard that tune a hundred times before and never realized where in fact it was from until now. The Tattershall was the same river that had saved him from the harper. The harper. And where was he now?

"Let's dance," Ainsy said, and pulled him to his feet.

Kern loved to dance. He clomped about the dance floor in his borrowed boots—just a tad too large for him— careful not to tread on his partner's feet. She was like a feather in his arms. One moment her hair was tickling his cheek, the next she was throwing her head back and laughing at the fun.

He saw Fion haul Wat to his feet and was surprised at the big man's lightness of foot. There was already a crowd of young men standing about, asking for a dance, but

Fion only shook her head, saying, "Later." Tolly still sat at the table. Beside him was a dark-haired girl with her head full of curls and bows that must be Sara. She had broad friendly features and was giggling as Tolly whispered in her ear. Tomtim, his face still bruised, but his spirits much recovered, caught Kern's eye and winked.

One tune led into another and the dancing went on. As the dance floor was so small, the folk took their turns on it, which was just as well since it gave them a chance to both catch their breath and fill up their mugs once more. The barmaids were kept busy running from tap to table, and standing behind the bar, drawing the pints, was a tall man with a wide grin who must, Kern decided, be the inn's proprietor, he looked so pleased.

Kern almost forgot his fear as he became caught up in the night's merriment. But when a hush fell over the crowd and he saw the tall harper working his way through the tables, instrument in hand, his good humor drained away. There was no forgetting that lean face. The knot in Kern's stomach drew tight again, and when the harper was settled on his stool and pulled the first chords from his harp, a deadly chill ran up the shapechanger's spine. There was no forgetting his touch on the harp either.

Slouching in his chair, Kern tried to keep from sight, but it seemed he need not have bothered. The harper played, a small smile tugging the corners of his mouth as he bent over his instrument. His eyes were mild as he looked over the crowd. He passed over Kern without a flicker of recognition. He saw me only in wolfshape, Kern thought. Why should he recognize me now as a man? Perhaps I'm still safe and the secret's mine alone.

And so it would seem.

The harper played one tune after the other with heart-stopping skill. The airs were poignant, tenderly measured, with harmonies that gave the impression that two or three instruments played, instead of one. The dance tunes had a stately grace to them, so that it was the heart that kept time to them, rather than the feet. Images formed in the minds of the listeners, one dissolving into the next as the music changed its moods. Harping and images coalesced into one experience so that one couldn't tell whether the ears heard or the eyes saw, they were so entwined.

Kern began to relax, for all his fears. His memories grew dim. His anger faded, replaced with a strange wonder. Ainsy leaned her head against his shoulder, her face flushed with pleasure. Throughout the Foxfire's common room, the folk scarcely breathed as the harper's magic carried them beyond its confines into a realm where only music held sway. Then a last chord rang and the folk began to stir. The harper looked out at the crowd.

"Would you have a tale?" he asked.

A murmur of approval ran the length of the room and Kern found himself nodding along with the others. The harper smiled.

"I have only the old tales," he said. "This one is from

Yurn, a land far to the south of Penenghay, where folk worship the sungod Uruth, rather than your own moon-lady Arn. The people of Yurn fear the moon, and with good reason, for in their land, there is safety only in the hours of daylight. At night, evil rules.

"Imagine, if you will, that among you dwelt men who were not truly men, who, in darkness and by the light of the moon, shed their human skins to walk the night as beasts, and as such, slay their neighbors, their kith and kin. The hours 'twixt sunset and dawn are long and strange, and who knows what walks the world when the night holds sway?"

He pulled a dramatic chord from his instrument that rang strange and eerie through the common room. Here and there folk shivered with a curious mixture of fear and delight. This was a man who could tell a tale, they thought, and some settled back to listen, while others leaned forward on the very edge of their chairs.

As the harper spoke, Kern could smell his own fear come creeping from his pores. The ale he was in the middle of swallowing tasted flat. He knows, he thought, but the harper paid him no heed. Harp music swelled, then died away into a trickle of soft sound.

"Listen to me," the harper said, "and I will tell you a tale. Here in the north you will hear it as you might a legend, but in the south, in Yurn where it had its birth, they tell it as history. Listen, and I will tell you the tale of Tascar, the Wehr-wulf."

Now his eyes were for Kern alone. They impaled him with their strength of will, stripped the manflesh to bare the wolf inside. *I know you,* they said. *I remember you.* Echoes of that hateful music that called forth the feragh hung in the air. *The hunt is not yet done,* the harper's eyes appeared to say. Then he looked away and began the tale.

Kern was bathed in a thin film of sweat. His shirt clung to his back and his throat was tight with emotion. What game did the harper play? He knew what Kern was. He *knew.* Yet he did nothing.

Suddenly the room was stifling. The heat of too many bodies was oppressive. Too many odors attacked his nostrils—sweat and smoke and stale beer. He needed to flee, but was rooted to his chair, spellbound by the lies the harper spun. The words speared him. The incidental music that the harper used to evoke moods wove the net that bound Kern. He could no more move from his chair than a pig could sail the air. He could only listen to the tale—the lies!—unfold. How village folk took in a stranger and how he betrayed them in his beastshape. How they hunted him long and hard, with hounds and silver weapons. And how, in the end, they slew him and ended his bloody threat, though not before many and many of them were slain themselves.

The harper ended his tale with the lament of the fox from the tune called "The Foxhunt." A last time he looked at Kern, his dark eyes promising terrors to come, and he smiled. The tale ended and the final chords of the lament echoed in a pregnant silence. Then the room erupted in a thunder of applause.

The harper nodded his thanks, eyes downcast modestly, and left his place by the hearth. As he made his way to the bar, ale was offered to him and whiskey, coins sparkled in the candlelight, folk slapped him on his shoulder, others pumped his hand.

"That was magic," Ainsy sighed at Kern's side.

He nodded wordlessly, gaze fixed on the harp that stood by the hearth. The harper was gifted. There was no denying that. His every word and phrase dripped magic, and when he played, his music had a life of its own. A life of its own. The silver-furred feragh reared in Kern's mind and he shuddered. Would it be waiting for him outside or along the way home?

He longed for his wolfshape. It was not that the wolf was so much stronger. Rather it had a better chance to flee. It knew the woods better, could run quicker, could hide more secretly, attack or defend with greater skill. He felt very exposed, sitting where he was, surrounded by strangers, clothing entrapping his limbs. But shapechanging was denied him for the nonce. He could not bring the wolf out amid this crowd, not with the harper's tale still ringing in their ears. His clothing would entangle the wolf limbs. There were too many of them. And there was . . .

"Are you all right?" Ainsy asked.

"A little tired."

"We should be going home."

Home, Kern thought, and tasted the word with bitter-sweet pleasure. Almost he'd had a home. Now it flitted just beyond his grasp, like a will-o'-the-wisp, glittering in the dusk, borne away by the harper's threat. He watched as Ainsy gathered the others and his sense of sorrow grew stronger. He looked away, to the bar where the harper stood. Their gazes clashed and Kern felt again the help-less rage of a trapped beast.

Damn him! Damn him anyway! What right did he have to torment him?

The harper looked from Kern to Ainsy and back. Smiling, he turned away. Kern's heart pounded against his ribs. No, he thought. Don't touch her. Almost he rose, there and then and damn the consequences. He needed to confront the harper and end it once and for all. But Ainsy was at his side, and when she touched his arm, love for her stole the edge from his intent and the moment was gone.

"Are you going to finish your ale?" she asked.

"I'm done with it."

"Why don't you bring the horses around front while I settle up our bill? I'll send Tolly along to give you a hand if I can drag him away from his sweetheart."

"I'll come with you, Master Kern," Wat said.

Outside, Kern's nostrils flared as he sifted the night air for the feragh's scent. His caution proved misplaced. There was nothing more dangerous nearby than a sleepy cat who blinked one eye open as they walked by. The dirt crunched under their boots. The stars were bright above, wheeling in their eternal dance. At the stables, the ostler brought out the two horses. He was grumpy and had no sooner handed the reins over to them than he turned and disappeared back into the stables.

"Were a scary story he told, weren't it, Master Kern?"

"Eh?"

Wat was holding the reins of one horse while Kern hitched the other to the cart.

"The harper. And his story."

Kern shrugged. "Did you like it?"

"Don't know. Do you think it was true, like he said it was? Are there really whe-we–"

"Werewolves."

Wat nodded. "Do you think they're real, Master Kern?"

Kern finished buckling the last strap and straightened.

"What do you think, Wat?"

"I think they might be."

"So do I. But not like the harper made them out to be. I don't think they're evil. Just different. Like . . ." He searched for an analogy. "Like the kimeyn."

"Do you believe in the kimeyn, Master Kern?"

Wat's eyes were alight with excitement.

"I'd have to. After all, they pulled me from the river, didn't they?"

"You remember them?"

Kern shook his head. "But who else was there?"

"It must have been them," Wat agreed. "And they stole

Miss Ainsy's pie and some ale while we were out looking at you." He scratched his chin as he worked through a thought. "I don't think they're evil either. Just tricksy. I'd dearly love to see them someday."

Kern smiled. "Perhaps someday you will. Let's get the horses around front."

The way home was uneventful. Tolly borrowed the one horse to see Sara home while the others went on ahead. Ainsy and Fion sat on the driver's seat of the cart. Kern and Wat took turns walking alongside and riding in the back with Tomtim. Much of the talk centered around the harper and his tale.

"I'd hate to meet one of those creatures on the road tonight," Fion said. "Or any night, for that matter."

"Master Kern says they're not always bad," Wat offered.

"All the tales I've heard say they are," Fion replied. "Besides, how would 'Master Kern' know?"

Tomtim shifted to a more comfortable position. Tapping some ash out of his pipe bowl, he thrust it back into his mouth and spoke around the stem. "The world beyond the valley's full of strange tales," he said. "The thing to remember about stories is that they're always based on something true."

"But *werewolves*? I suppose you believe in kimeyn as well?"

"Who leaves a saucer of cream out for them, Fion? You or I?"

"That's just a habit. I got that from me mum. Besides, the cream's still there in the morning."

"Always?"

Fion laughed. "When the cat hasn't got at it. Or Stram, for that matter. Next you'll be telling me to leave out a chunk of raw meat for the werewolf. Wouldn't *that* give the cat and dog something to fight over?"

Tomtim shrugged. "Still, there's things in the world for which there's no easy explanation. Broom and heather! When you wend the roads like I have, you learn to be careful about such things."

"I wish you'd all stop talking about that," Ainsy said. "You're giving me the creeps."

Kern, who was taking his turn walking by the cart, sighed. And what would you think if you knew what your love was? he asked her silently. He cast a glance back over his shoulder. The wind told him that the feragh was nowhere behind them, but that didn't reassure him. The harper's promise had been plain enough. When would he come? And how?

For Kern, the night was tense with danger. On one side of the road, the river murmured; on the other, the Tamwood creaked and groaned to itself. They were familiar sounds. Kern had heard their like a thousand times and better. He saw bats hunting, a badger rooting at an old log, a hare in among the underbrush, watching them with fear-wide eyes. All was as it should be, except Kern couldn't shake the memory of the harper from him. Thus the familiar became strange and he started at every sound, stared at every hint of movement.

Not until they pulled into the Tinker's courtyard did he feel some measure of security return. But as he stabled the horse and made his way into the inn, another concern rose in him. What if the harper struck at him through Ainsy or one of the others? He'd kept that fear at the back of his mind, but standing in the courtyard, feeling the close warmth of the inn and its occupants all around him, it surfaced stronger than ever. Must he go? Could he risk their lives by staying?

He looked back the way they'd come. What did I do for you to hate me so? he asked the distant harper. But he knew the question was only so much rhetoric. He was a shapechanger and that was reason enough. Men never needed more. It was simple difference that woke the anger in them. Did he have a hunched back rather than the shapechanging gift, they'd hate him still, though not so much. Not enough to hunt and kill.

Stram came sauntering across the yard and thrust his nose into Kern's hand.

"You and I are friends now," he said as he ruffled Stram's ears. "If only it were always so easy."

Sighing, he went into the inn.

Later, he lay with Ainsy curled in the crook of his arm. Sleep eluded him. He looked down at Ainsy's face and smoothed the hair from her cheek. Their lovemaking had been tender tonight, touched, on Kern's part, by the poignant awareness that it might soon be no more. He knew he should leave, be gone before the harper struck, but couldn't. What lay ahead for him? More wandering, friendless days and nights, one dissolving into the other. And if he remained? Could he bear to see Ainsy, to see any of them hurt because of him?

Tuiloch, he said to himself. Fion had named the harper for him. Tuiloch. He hated the name. If only there were some way to carry the battle to him. But with his power and the feragh. . . . His power. The harp. Excitement stirred in Kern. The harp was his strength, but his weakness as well. Without the harp, where then his power? And without power. . . .

A grim smile played on Kern's lips. If he could find a way to destroy Tuiloch's harp, the harper would be a threat no more. Yet how to get at the instrument? Surely it would be well guarded. The feragh and the stars alone knew what other maleficent creatures safeguarded it for him. But if he could find a way . . .

When Kern fell asleep at last, he dreamed of broken harps and wolves that chased a dark-clothed harper, as hounds might a stag.

Eighth...

Busy days followed their night out. The immediacy of Kern's quarrel with Tuiloch and his harping grew dim amid concerns of the inn and the closeness of the communal unit into which he was being drawn. There was so much to do about the place as they readied for the winter months that the days tumbled into one another and two weeks passed in what seemed like the space of one.

Tomtim once said, Tolly told Kern one day, and Ainsy always held it as true, that the less you depended on others, the better off your lot would be. It was the tinker in him speaking, who knew well the need for tightening his belt when folk would neither buy his goods nor bring him work for mending. When the town sheriff bade him shift on and there was nothing put away in the wagon's larder. When the road was empty and long. Then it was time to set snares in the woods and gather up the wild roots.

The tinker in him knew, and the tinker in Ainsy acted. So the inn was run as self-sufficiently as possible, with whatever trading and buying that needed to be done kept to a minimum. Luxuries they could do without, but not necessities. What work was required, they did themselves. What food or comforts they wished for, they grew or produced for themselves. It made for hard work, but they knew pride in it and lacked for little.

In those two weeks then, with winter almost at their door, they were busier than ever. Kern worked shoulder to shoulder with Wat and Tolly as they prepared the inn and outbuildings against the rough weather to come. Loose boards and shingles were mended or replaced, calking was done where it was needed, storm shutters were fitted to the windows. The chimneys were swept and any loose stones were set securely against their neighbors once more. The privies were cleaned and the refuse removed to the far end of the garden where it was buried in trenches. In the spring it would be turned into the garden before sowing.

The last of the hay was pitched into the loft. Two of the pigs were butchered and their meat preserved. What grain they'd need for the next few months was threshed. Firewood was laid in, kindling chopped. With Ainsy and Fion, Kern rolled fleece in the evenings, jarred preserves and jams, corked wine, casked ale, began new brews with the last of the summer hops. Soon the winter storms would come roaring down in earnest, and closed off from the rest of the world, they would have only what they'd provided for themselves.

With Tomtim, Kern worked some afternoons in the

small shed alongside the barn that served as the tinker's smithy. The doors and windows were propped open for ventilation, but the fire roared, and what with its heat and that of their laboring bodies, they were never cold. Mostly they worked at mending tools and kitchenware, both their own and what the neighbors brought. But while Kern repaired a nicked ax head or fitted a new handle to a pot, Tomtim often worked on his tinker blades.

They were Tomtim's pride and joy—fourteen-inch blades set in handles of briar. The making of each knife was a long process, and by the end of the winter, if he had a dozen for sale, he'd consider it a good season's work. He began with a soft bar of iron, heated it until it was red, then folded it over, the hammer ringing on the hot metal with a satisfying clatter that could be heard as far as the river. By the time a blade was finished, it would have been folded at least twenty times—the end result being a blade with thousands of layers in its metal. Then he tempered it, with wax or clay, six times, until the cutting edge would never lose its sharpness, while the back of the blade remained flexible enough to absorb blows. Both strong and resilient, tinker blades seldom shattered, no matter what stress was put on them.

None of the work that Kern did about the inn was new to him. He had helped out at many a holding and farm in preparation for winter. But here, it was different. He did not toil so much *for* them as *with* them. What surprised him most was the ease with which he joined the familial aspects of the inn folk. He was never a stranger with them. Only sometimes in the evenings, while taking a last walk around the inn yard before bed, did a feeling of disquiet steal over him.

Staring into the darkness, he'd smell the forest and, inside, the wolf would stir. And with that stirring came a cascade of memories and fears. The joy he felt was too perfect to last. He tried to keep his worries at bay, afraid that by giving them space in his mind, he gave them life. But it was no use. The wolf was still a part of him, could still divorce him from Ainsy and the others did they learn exactly what he was. And somewhere out in the night, down the valley, was the harper.

At times like this the threat of the harper's promise was a palpable thing. It had a life of its own and there was no way he could control his reaction to it. And this was exactly what Tuiloch wanted. Kern would ask himself: What drove the harper? Could Kern himself forestall the attack? How to get at the harp?

There were no easy answers. He couldn't walk up to him the next time he was in Hay-on-Pen and put his boot through the instrument. Tuiloch was a bard and revered as such by the village folk—even by Ainsy and the others at the Tinker. For Kern to strike at Tuiloch, without displaying just cause, would be sacrilege in their eyes. What then? Wait until he had Tuiloch alone in the woods? Take the chance that he could destroy the harp before Tuiloch called up its guardian? And if he wasn't swift enough? Kern shook his head. Damned if he did and damned if he didn't.

Perhaps Tuiloch would simply leave him alone. Perhaps he'd stay in Bridgeford over the winter and travel on north in the spring. Perhaps he'd gone through Yern Pass and had left the valley behind already. Kern bared his teeth in a mirthless grin. Of course! And perhaps the moon would drift down from the sky and bear him away.

Many nights Kern returned to the inn with his thoughts as sour as vinegar and only Ainsy's warmth could dispell his gloom. He'd be caught for long moments, between loving her and the fear of losing her, until their lovemaking swallowed his mood. There was more than solace in Ainsy's arms. There was an indefinable oneness that made his burdens seem like so much chaff in the wind. And he knew, could he only bare his heart to her, take the chance, that the fears could well be gone forever. But at these times he would only see Tera's face, superimposed over Ainsy's features. The old lover and his parents, and the moment would be gone. He simply did not have the courage.

Then one morning he woke and knew. Something had changed. Tuiloch had returned from Bridgeford and they would meet again. He was not surprised, lying beside Ainsy and staring out the window at the leaden autumn skies. The clouds held snow. And the day held . . . harping.

"Come," it said. "We will meet, you and I, and one of

us will spill our red blood on the snow. Which will it be?" The harping mocked him as it slipped the strains of a taunting jig into its discordance. Kern could feel the blood run cold in his veins. His hackles rose. "What color a werewolf's blood?" the harping asked. "The hue of his fur? Or darker still?"

Kern eased Ainsy's head from his shoulder and padded to the window, half expecting Tuiloch to be standing outside it, fingers pulling the bitter tune from his harp's strings, his face a mask of mocking lies. But no one was there. Kern shivered suddenly, feeling the stone floor cold against his feet. A last echo of harpmusic drifted from beyond the window—or within his soul. Sighing, Kern turned and made his way back to the bed. He looked down at Ainsy's face and smoothed the curls from her cheek.

In a way he was relieved that the moment was come. But if he should lose her. . . . He would sooner lose his life. He glanced back at the window. Frost curlicued in the corners and he imagined shapes in the ice patterns. The wolf running. Harpstrings. The feragh's muzzle, lips drawn back to reveal its long canines.

"You will not find me such an easy prey this time, harper," he said.

Ainsy stirred and her eyelids fluttered open. "Did . . . did you say something?" she asked around a yawn.

Kern shook his head. "I was just mumbling."

She looked past him to the window.

"Arn! It's still early." Lifting her arms, she drew him back onto the bed. "Too early to be thinking of getting up. . . ."

With an effort, Kern set aside his inner tumult and let her pull him down into an embrace.

It started snowing just before noon. Kern and Tomtim came from the smithy, heading for the kitchen, and met Tolly hauling in the last of the wood loads. While Tomtim went on, Kern gave Tolly a hand with the wood. They put the mare in the barn with a bucketful of oats in her manger and followed Tomtim's tracks to the inn. The bootprints were almost half full by the time the two of them reached the kitchen door.

"Be a foot or worse by nightfall," Tolly complained, stamping the snow off his boots. He hung his coat by the door and went to stand by the hearth, rubbing his hands together. "I met Haddy while I was out getting the wood," he added. "He had a weird tale to tell."

"What's that?" Fion asked.

She was filling soup bowls and handing them to Wat, who carried them carefully to the table.

"Old Yan Buther was found dead outside his barn this morning."

He had everyone's attention. Yan Buther kept a small farm this side of Hay-on-Pen where he ran a few head of cattle, some sheep, and put in a good barley crop that was sold out of the valley to the brewers in Tigshire every year. The brewers swore by Penenghay barley and even had valley birch shipped over the mountain for the quality it gave to their whiskey distilling, maintaining that the two went hand in hand.

"Yan's dead?" Ainsy was cutting bread and set the knife down on the cutting board. "How did he die?"

"Torn apart by some sort of animal is the word going around." Tolly turned away from the fire. "His missus never even knew he'd left the house. She woke to find the bed beside her empty, went out to the kitchen, and saw him from the window, lying in front of the barn. Haddy was talking to Lovell, who spent the night at the Buther farm. *He* says Yan was killed by wolves."

Tomtim shook his head. "There's not been wolves in the valley for a hundred years or better. Not since my granddad's time."

"Maybe so," Tolly replied. "But what's to stop them from coming back? Lovell swears he heard them howling last night. And remember the harper from the Foxfire? *He* said he saw a wolf in the valley—not more'n two weeks ago."

"Wolves don't attack a man without reason," Tomtim said.

Tolly shrugged. "Who knows what wolves do, or why?"

"You sound like a townsman speaking of a tinker," Tomtim said, and spat into the fire.

Ainsy stepped between them. "Don't argue. Broom and heather! Think of poor Mrs. Buther. We'll have to do something for her. And ourselves. . . ." She looked from Tolly to Kern. "The livestock . . . ?"

"There's no wolf alive'll get into the inn or barn," Tolly said. "The repairs are all done. It might be a good idea to go out in pairs, though. At night, that is."

Kern said nothing. The buildings were protection enough against wild beasts. But what of harpmagic and the creatures it could raise? Would a wooden door be any hindrance to the feragh? Or if the harper's magic simply lifted the latch to let the monster in? For Kern put no credence to this tale of wolves slaying their neighbor. He could sense the harper's hand in it as surely as if he'd seen the deed done himself. The killing was tied to Tuiloch—and through the harper, to himself.

He remembered the harper's tale of the werewolf and an icy premonition stirred in the pit of his stomach. The blood drained from his face. He thought he knew what Tuiloch was about. One senseless death. Perhaps a few others. Then the tale of werewolf would be whispered about and folk would regard each other with suspicion, no matter that they'd known each other all their lives. And they would look to strangers and they would wonder. . . . At some point, speculation would become fact. Then silver coins and torcs, bracelets and candlesticks, would be melted down into weapons. Perhaps in the same smithy where he'd worked side by side with Tomtim. And then the hunt would begin again, though not conducted by the harper and his magics. He would have others do his hunting for him.

"It's a bad thing, isn't it, Miss Ainsy?" Wat was saying.

"It's a terrible thing!" she replied. "Such a senseless death. Is anything being done to hunt the creatures down?"

Tolly shrugged. "The snows covered any traces the hounds might have followed."

Kern looked from face to face and read the wolf fear in them. What was it about his grey brothers that filled people with such terror? They spoke of a pack numbering thirty or more, when such was never the case. A pack of twelve wolves was extraordinarily large. Folk told tales of atrocities that only men were capable of and laid the blame on a wolf. Not that wolves were gentle creatures, incapable of violent actions. They were the rulers of the forest, fierce and implacable when aroused. But first there must be a threat of some sort. . . .

Suddenly Kern was aware of Tomtim watching him. Their gazes locked and a nervous twitch coiled up Kern's spine. Did Tomtim know? What did he remember of that night by the burning wagon? Kern could read nothing in the old tinker's eyes. Tomtim looked away then, and the moment was gone, though the nervousness remained.

"We'll go up to the Buther farm after lunch," Ainsy said, putting the platter of bread on the table. The soup was served all around. "I've a couple of meat pies we can leave with the missus and we can see if there's any work that needs to be done about the place."

"She had a cousin up Glenhaven way," Fion said. "We should send word to her. And to Yan's brother in Bridgeford."

Ainsy nodded. "If it hasn't already been done."

The talk around the table was subdued throughout the meal. Outside, the snow still fell, piling up against the buildings, drifting across the yard. Kern could still see the fear in all of them. It was subtle, more in the backs of their eyes than in their faces. They all knew what it was like to be wintered in the deep snows, cut off from all neighbors. And if there was a menace abroad, a wolf pack. . . . Kern sighed. There *was* a menace abroad. Only it walked on two legs instead of four and was cloaked in the near-sacred flesh of a bard.

The harp was the key. It must be destroyed, and destroyed quickly; before more deaths were laid at the wolf's den, before talk turned from a natural threat of wolves running wild to more supernatural speculations. Such as shapechangers. Werewolves. Himself. Yet how was he to go about it?

For an instant he heard again a distant echo of mocking harp notes, skittering through his mind like a cascade of stones rattling down a hillside. He knows, Kern thought. Tuiloch knows. And if the harper was on his guard, what chance did Kern have to destroy the harp? Little. Or none. Still, he meant to try. The harpmusic returned at that moment, derisive and sly. Kern looked around the table, but no one gave notice of hearing anything. It was only him. In his mind. Tuiloch's scorn clotting in his mind like spoiled milk.

After lunch, Tolly and Kern dragged a sleigh out of the shed behind the barn and hitched the mares to it. The snow was thick about their ankles as they went back and forth between the inn and sleigh, loading pies, blankets, candles, and ale into the back. At last they were ready to go. Wat and Tomtim stayed behind, waving goodbye. The old tinker returned to his work in the smithy with Wat trailing in his footsteps, Stram at the big man's heels.

Kern looked back until the inn was lost from sight. The fields were white around them, the evergreens low slung with the weight of snow that bowed their branches groundward. The mares' harnesses jingled with bells and still the snow fell. Kern imagined the white powder under his paws, his guard hairs sleek with wet snow, his underfur warm and untouched, the wind on his face, his breath wreathing his muzzle. For the wolf there was nothing grim about winter. Only game was scarcer. But he'd always been a good hunter. Hunter. He thought of the reason they were on their way to the Buther farm. Against those thoughts floated a memory of the night he'd rescued Tomtim from the brigands. Again he tasted the hot blood in his mouth and shuddered. What had their thoughts been, with his wolf jaws at their throats, tearing the life from them? And this Yan Buther. Slain on his own farm. . . .

He shook his head. Such thinking did him no good. Yet he couldn't free himself from the memories. They rose stark and substantial, creeping up from his subconscious with a will of their own. No matter that he might have come to terms with them, justified his actions as best he could, nothing could change what had been done.

He had slain men in his wolfshape, as surely as any werewolf of legend, whatever his motives. The memories were there, imprinted in his mind for all time. He doubted that he'd ever be free of them.

There was quite a crowd gathered at the Buther farm when they arrived. Kern was introduced to so many broad-faced, grave folk that he soon lost track of the names. They were all farm folk, come from neighboring holdings to do what they could to ease the widow's grief. Honest, hardworking folk who stood about shocked at what had befallen one of their own. Kern heard the words *senseless killing* so often that they grated on his nerves. There was talk, too, of raising a hunt and combing the woods for the wolf pack. Go out, Kern thought, and you'll find nothing but shadows and snow. Tuiloch would have left nothing for them to track him by. But he could say nothing, could only nod in agreement when someone looked his way or he was asked a question.

He looked often to the door of the barn and the ground

before it. The yard was patterned with footprints that new snow was rapidly filling in. There was no sign of what had befallen the farmer last night. No track, no scent. No blood on the white snow. Still, Kern could sense the harper's nearness and he longed to be away.

There was little to be done about the farm. Yan Buther had been a conscientious man and whatever had needed doing to prepare for the coming winter months had been done. So Kern milled in the farmyard with the others, but didn't take his turn going into the high-beamed kitchen of the farmhouse. What could he say to the widow? I'm sorry? The words would be meaningless coming from a stranger. So he waited until Ainsy and Fion came out, their faces drawn, eyes sad, as they got into the sleigh. Tolly drifted over and they started up for home.

"She's bearing up well," Fion said.

Ainsy nodded and searched for Kern's hand, squeezing it when she found it.

"It makes you think, doesn't it?" she said. "Death. It's always there, just around the corner. You try and ignore it, pretend that only other people die, until you're faced with it. Seeing Lora Buther and the bleak look in her eyes. . . ." She sighed. "You know what I thought? Poor Lora. But also, thank Arn it wasn't one of mine. What a terrible thing to think of."

"I think we all feel like that when we're confronted with death," Kern said. "It's not unnatural."

"It makes me feel selfish. Wicked."

"It shouldn't," Kern said. "You don't mean it as an ill wish."

"I suppose not."

She rubbed at her eye with her free hand. Kern had closed his fingers about the other.

Ninth...

Wat came out to meet them as they pulled into the inn yard. His face was split with a broad grin that was a sharp contrast to the long faces of those in the sleigh.

"Miss Ainsy!" he called. "We've a guest!"

"Who'd be out in this weather?" she asked.

Before Wat could answer, Kern felt his gaze drawn to the doorway of the inn and saw him standing there. Tuiloch. The harper. He met Kern's eye with a measuring look and smiled condescendingly. Then he started out from the doorway. Kern stifled the sudden desire to lash out at him. What good would it do? Ainsy and the others would think he was mad. But what was Tuiloch doing here?

The harper gave Ainsy and Fion a hand down from the sleigh while Kern looked stupidly on. Tuiloch bent over Ainsy's hand, lips brushing it.

"Well met, lady. And if I may be so bold, welcome to your own inn."

Ainsy blushed. She was unused to such attention,

especially from someone as important as the harper. Fion looked from them to Kern and frowned.

"When I first saw you at the Foxfire," Tuiloch continued, "I knew I must know you better. Unfortunately, I had already promised to visit a friend in Bridgeford and had to put off my visit until now."

"You came . . . just to see me?"

Tuiloch smiled. "Does that surprise you, Morain?"

No one called her Morain. At least not twice. But hearing it come from the harper's lips, it took on a pleasing sound. She felt flustered and glanced at Fion, not seeing the warning lights that flashed in the dark-haired woman's eyes.

"While your retainers put away the sleigh, will you allow me to see you inside?" He offered her his arm.

"I . . . ah. That is. . . ."

He took her hand and, placing it on his arm, walked her to the door. In the sleigh, Kern sat numbly, watching their receding backs. Retainers. Retainers! He understood now what the harper was doing here. It wasn't enough to set the valley folk against him. Tuiloch would play a subtler game than that. Kern's knuckles whitened as he gripped the side of the sleigh.

"Kern!" Fion said. "Are you going to let him get away with that?"

He blinked and focused on her face. "Get away with what?" he asked bitterly.

"He means to steal Ainsy from you."

Fion had read the harper's intentions with as much perception as Kern. In that moment, she forgot that the man was a harper, forgot how much she'd enjoyed his music. She saw only a stranger trying to disrupt the closeness of her family.

"A man like that," she said, "cares only for himself. He'd stay how long? The winter? A week? A night? He'll break her heart."

"It's her heart," Kern said.

He knew what Fion was driving at. But from the moment the harper had spoken, Ainsy hadn't even glanced at Kern. What hurt the most was that there was no magic afoot here, no harping. Only the man's charm. Tall and handsome, he was a harper. He was important.

"But Kern. . . ." Fion's voice was filled with disappointment.

He lifted his big hands. "What am I compared to him, Fion? As common as dirt. No," he added, stilling her protest. "That's what I am."

"But she loves you!"

Kern nodded. "So I should trust her, shouldn't I? I can't claim ownership of her."

"But if you do nothing. . . ."

"What should I do? Hit him?" How he longed to. "I'm a simple man, Fion. That man could charm anyone into doing anything." Even without using his harpmagic, Kern was beginning to realize. "There could be no contest between us. None that I could win."

Fion nodded glumly. Tuiloch had stepped in and spoken and the world had fallen away for Ainsy, leaving just her and the harper in it. Arn above! He'd called her Morain and she'd smiled. So she realized what Kern was saying. What *could* he do? Jealousy was a sharp blade that cut both ways. Did he say anything, he'd look the fool and become even less in Ainsy's eyes.

Perhaps they were jumping to conclusions. Except the suddenness of the encounter, and the depth of it, frightened Fion. In just a few words and motions, Tuiloch had blinded Ainsy's heart. Fion knew that type of man. They'd had all too many patrons exactly like him. Only usually they came smiling around her. She'd been stung only the once—the first time. Oh, how it had hurt. But before the man had cast her away like so much chaff, there had been nothing that he could say that she didn't hang on to every word of, no action of his that could be faulted.

"Go on in," Kern said to her and Tolly. "I'll see to the sleigh and horses."

Fion sighed and nodded to Tolly, who'd sat silent throughout the entire exchange. Wat had long since followed Ainsy and the harper into the inn.

"What's wrong with you two?" Tolly asked Fion as they walked to the door, snow crunching under their boots. "You're making a mountain out of nothing. I'd think you'd be tickled pink to have the harper—the harper!— staying with us. Or"—he glanced at her slyly—"are you just jealous that it's Ainsy he likes, rather than you?"

Fion stopped to look at him. She seemed about to say something, then shook her head. Leaving him standing in the snow, she went on alone.

"Fion!" he called. "I didn't mean—"

"Leave it be!"

"But. . . ."

"Leave it!"

She vanished into the inn and Tolly stood, shaking his own head. What had gotten into her? He glanced back at Kern. What had gotten into both of them? It was beyond him.

Kern was gentle with the horses, rubbing them down in their stalls and feeding them each handfuls of oats mixed with bits of dried apple. But as he went to hang up the harnesses, a savage mood came over him. He threw them against the wall, then ground them under his heel. He should have known. He should have expected something like this from that night in the Foxfire and the look Tuiloch had given Ainsy. He shouldn't have spent two weeks around the inn when he could have been after that damned harper. Now. . . . Now! He snarled. Again Tuiloch was in control—without even the use of his magic, unless it was magic that gave him his features and his glamour.

Kern saw it all now. Tuiloch meant to attack from both sides—turning not only the valley against Kern with his werewolf lies, but coming between Kern and the only joy he'd known as well. What would be the harper's next move? Could he destroy the harp before it? Though what use was that? He had Ainsy ensorcelled now. And he need only fashion another harp.

It was all too much for Kern. He ran from the barn, into the snow. Beyond sight of the inn he stripped his clothing from him and willed the wolfshape onto his bones. Then he loped into the wind, his heart pounding with rage. He lifted his head and howled at the storm, a long mournful sound that echoed all the bitterness swelling inside him. Then he raced on, determined to burn the anger from him. He could not chance his rage clouding his reason. In this struggle with Tuiloch he'd need all his wits if he hoped to survive.

Inside the inn, it was worse than Fion had feared. Tuiloch had Ainsy by the large hearth in the common room and was speaking persuasively to her, his voice earnest and low, his hand on her knee. Ainsy's face was aglow with wonder. And why not? Fion thought bitterly. It wasn't every day that a harper came courting, his tongue like honey, his every word a poem.

She heard a sound then, from outside, a wild keening cry, and her blood chilled. Her eyes were on the harper and she saw him smile. It was a wolf's cry they'd heard. Why does it amuse him? Fion asked herself. She watched Ainsy shiver and lean close to the harper. His arm went around her shoulder and Fion turned away. The cold in her veins wouldn't leave her. She saw Tolly and Wat staring out the window into the falling snow, listening for a repetition of the cry. Only Tomtim appeared unmoved, or at least, the howl awoke a different reaction in him.

Sadness, Fion thought. The wolf's cry makes him sad. But why? She went and sat beside him.

"What is it?"° she asked, her voice low and carrying no further than his ear.

Tomtim shook his head. "Nothing," he said.

He looked away so that she wouldn't see that the word was a lie.

Kern returned just as supper was being set on the table. His clothes were soaked. Snow turned to water and dripped from them. Steam hung about his shoulders as the warm air of the inn swirled about him. Ainsy looked at him like he was a stranger, her gaze going from him to the harper as though measuring the one against the other. Whatever emotion Kern felt, he kept hidden. He nodded and smiled and went to change, returning to sit at the table in dry clothes.

At first an awkward silence hung over the table.

"Where did you go?" Fion asked him.

"For a walk. It's quite a night out there."

Fion shook her head. He seemed so calm. But there was something flickering in the back of his eyes.

"Storms," Tuiloch said musingly. "There's something about them that brings out a wildness inside us, don't you think? Awakens the beast within, so to speak."

Ainsy hung on his every word. Looking at her, Fion wanted to grab her by the shoulders and shake her until her teeth rattled. Wake up! she wanted to scream into her ear. Can't you see what he's doing to you? She realized something else at that moment. Looking from the harper to Ainsy, who sat as quiet as a snake-charmed bird, she knew it wasn't Ainsy he wanted. He did this to torment Kern. But why? What was between them? As far as she knew they'd never met before that night at the Foxfire, and they certainly hadn't spoken to each other then. Was it simply the natural antagonism that sometimes sprang up between two strangers for no apparent reason, other than that it was? Or something else?

"They are like music," Kern was saying to the harper. "Only a storm is a part of the world, unlike music that needs a man to create it."

"You dislike music?" Tuiloch asked, framing the question so that it seemed he was asking Kern if he was a molester of children.

Kern shook his head. "Not I. But I think I prefer the music of the wind in the trees or howling on a night like this, the sound of water falling over rocks, or the sea, to anything most men might pull from an instrument. Too few musicians play from the heart. Too many of them concentrate solely on technique, or form, or on impressing their audience, forgoing the origin and essence of the music." Kern tapped his chest as he repeated himself. "The heart, harper. The heart."

"Music should be controlled," Tuiloch began.

"Surely," Kern said. "To a degree. But to do what?"

"To bring pleasure to those who listen."

"Or pain."

Fion looked from one to the other. There was another conversation underlying what she was listening to, but she couldn't grasp it. She just knew it was there.

"You have heard me play. Which do I bring?"

"Lies," Kern said blandly.

The harper's face went still and for long moments it seemed that no one breathed around the table.

"What do you mean?" Tuiloch said at last.

Fion leaned forward, her meal forgotten. She glanced at Ainsy and saw her brow creased in a frown. What in Arn's name was Kern playing at? Surely he knew Ainsy well enough by now to know that he'd get nowhere antagonizing the harper. In her present state, Ainsy would defend Tuiloch against all comers.

Kern laughed. "You take me too seriously, harper. Or perhaps you take your music too seriously. What can it be but lies? You play a tune and someone laughs, another and they weep. What does it mean? Only that you deceived their reason long enough to play with their emotions. For surely . . . when you play a lament, does someone weep because they are sad themselves, or because your music tells them that it is sad?"

Now Tuiloch smiled as well. "Yet you said you liked music . . . Do you enjoy being lied to?"

"You weren't listening to me. I simply said that your music was made up of lies. Not all music. Not the music that comes from the heart."

Again the stillness settled across Tuiloch's features. It seemed that Ainsy was about to speak, but the harper shook his head.

"You have a roundabout method of insulting someone," he said. "Perhaps you'd care to show me this *heart* music after supper?"

Kern shook his head. "Not I." He lifted his big hands. "These are too clumsy for music, don't you think?"

Tuiloch shrugged.

The rest of the meal passed in relative silence. Afterward, while Kern remained in the kitchen, Tuiloch played for the others in the common room. Kern smiled as he listened to him play. He could hear the harper striving for depth, for heart, with his music, but it was something he didn't have. Kern had remembered that from his night in the Foxfire. The harping had been wondrous and otherworldly and left him gasping, but later, thinking of it, he'd realized that it had only toyed with him, not spoken heart to heart as music should. He knew the others could hear it as well, for all Tuiloch's efforts to prove otherwise.

It was a small victory for Kern and one that meant little, save for bolstering his own confidence. Unlike the rest of the inn folk, he knew the other music that Tuiloch could call up from his heart—but it was a music that he wouldn't play. Not now. Not yet.

Later on, as they were all readying for bed, Ainsy came up to him.

"How could you?" she demanded.

"Could I what?"

"Badger Tuiloch like you did. He was kind enough to come out here in this storm to play for us, and you—the way you spoke to him at supper. . . ."

Words failed her for a moment and Kern felt his heart go out to her. It hurt him terribly to hear her defending the harper, but from her point of view, it was Kern who was in the wrong. And there was nothing he could do without completely alienating her from him.

"Ainsy, I. . . ."

"You upset him, you know that, don't you? But that was what you were trying to do. And yet, for all the hurt he must have felt at your meanness, he still played for us. Could you hear the sadness in his music? Are you proud of your mocking? What in Arn's name possessed you to do that?"

"His music," Kern asked. "Was it the same as the night in the Foxfire?"

"What? No. Of course not. How could it be, upset as he was?"

"And the difference. Was it in his playing, or in the way you heard it?"

"It was. . . ." She frowned. "What difference does it make?"

But suddenly she knew what difference it made. She looked down at Kern's arms and saw the bundle of blankets he held.

"What are you doing with those?"

"I'm going to make my bed. In the barn. With Wat. Good night, Ainsy."

"The barn? But, Kern. . . ."

He shook off her hand. Without another word, he turned and went out the door, closing it softly behind him. Outside, the night was crisp, the sky clear. The snow had ceased an hour or so ago and the whole world was transformed into a magical realm, glistening in the starlight for as far as the eye could see. But the beauty of it brought Kern no joy. He heard the door open behind him and Ainsy calling to him. Sighing, he walked off across the inn yard.

"Kern!"

She took a step out the door, but a hand on her arm stopped her.

"You'll catch your death of cold going out like that," Tuiloch said. He looked past her to where Kern disappeared into the barn. "Was he bothering you?"

"Was he—" Ainsy turned and shrugged off his hand. "No, he *wasn't* bothering me. We were just . . . just. . . ."

His eyes caught hers and she felt a sudden weight in her limbs. It was like sinking into a bog, only she was falling forward, it seemed, drowning in his pale orbs, like a fly trapped in honey.

"Morain," he said softly, speaking her name like a charm.

She blinked at the use of it. It held none of the pleasure that it had earlier. How could it ever have held pleasure? It grated on the ears. She found he was holding her by the shoulders, the long slim fingers pale against the dark green print of her smock. She lifted her hand and brushed his grip aside.

"My name's Ainsy," she said. "And I'm going to bed. Please get out of my way. You can sit up all night in the common room if you like, or go to your room, it makes no difference to me. Just leave me alone."

She pushed by him and stomped off to her room. Closing the door behind her, she thought of Kern when her hand was on the bolt, and hesitated. Then she thought of Tuiloch and shot the bolt home. The room seemed small to her tonight. Small, or was it just lonely? She wanted to go out to the barn and ask Kern to forgive her meanness, her blindness, but didn't have the courage to face the harper again. She knew he'd still be out there. Just sitting in the common room, staring at the hallway that led here to her room.

"Broom and bloody heather! What in Arn's name came over me?" she asked.

The room remained silent, accusing her with its loneliness. Thinking back on the afternoon and evening, she was mortified. How could she have acted the way she did? Arn! She didn't even know the man and she'd been throwing herself all over him from the moment he'd come to the side of the sleigh.

Limply, she fell onto the bed and wrung the comforter with her fists, her knuckles going white. Tears started up in her eyes and ran hotly down her cheek.

"Oh, Kern. Kern."

What if he left during the night? Cheeks glistening, she sat up. She shouldn't take the chance. She should go to him right now. This minute. But then she heard the sound of soft harping start up in the common room and she pressed her face back against the comforter. The music, quiet as it was, wormed its way insidiously into her heart. She was white with fear, every limb trembling. She couldn't—couldn't!—go out there and face Tuiloch. Every note was like a tiny thorn driven into her soul. She smelled something weird in the air, then realized it was her own fear, seeping from her pores. Her smock clung wetly to her breasts and back.

"Oh, Kern!"

Too late to call him now. He was only across the inn yard, but with that harping between them, he might as well be across the world. Yet, had she seen Kern then, his own cheeks wet with tears, his own heart pounding as he listened to the weird harping, she would have damned the consequences and gone to him, harper or no harper. But as it was, she thought Kern hated her, hated herself for how she'd been today, and could only tug fistfuls of her bedclothes in her hands and weep.

In the common room, Tuiloch played thoughtfully, his mind only half on his music. They'd surprised him, the both of them. The shapechanger with his talk of hearts and music. He pulled a discordance from his instrument as he went over the conversation. He was surprised at how much that had troubled him. What does he know? he asked himself. He is nothing. Less than a man. What can he know of music? Yet Kern had cut to the heart of the matter and his words lay in Tuiloch's soul like bitter fruits, spoiled and rotting. And the girl. He'd had her so wrapped up that magic had hardly been needed. How had she broken free of his spell?

He shrugged and played a stronger tune. The end results would be the same. He would merely play the game more subtly than ever. Before he was finished, they'd be at each other's throats. And then, only then, would he end it to emerge the winner. As he always did. But before that ending came, the shapechanger would learn what it meant to spoil a mage's hunt. Before this was over, the shapechanger would beg his gods, if gods his kind had, to have died back on that ridge under the feragh's claws. That was a promise. This game would not be spoiled.

Smiling to himself, Tuiloch began a new tune. And

outside, as he played and his notes hung like sparks in the air, a figure of silver fur and monstrous proportions gathered shape in the moonlight.

Kern lay awake for hours, listening to the harpmusic drift across the inn yard. The walls of the barn and inn offered no hindrance to it, provided no barrier. It was as loud as though the harper sat on a bale of hay next to him. Restlessly, Kern waited for it to stop. He twisted and turned, trying to find a position that wasn't too comfortable, lest he fall asleep, but wasn't too bothersome either. He was waiting for the harping to stop, for once he was sure the harper was asleep, he meant to make his try for the instrument. Now. Tonight. But Tuiloch played on and Kern, fretting, could only listen.

It seemed to ring in his head, reverberating between his ears until he gritted his teeth together. He pressed his face into the straw, hands over his ears, and willed it to be gone. But still it played on. As loud as ever. Insidious as the refrain to a melody that might stick in your mind, no matter how you tried to dispel it. Kern tried to think of other things to take his mind from it.

He thought of Ainsy alone in their room. Their room! That was what it had become until Tuiloch's arrival. And now . . . the way she'd been with him tonight twisted like a knife inside him. Emotion tightened his chest, shaped what felt like a stone in the pit of his stomach. He had but one hope to hang on to, as a drowning man might grasp a floating spar as the sea washed over him. When he'd left the inn, she'd not seemed so ensorcelled by the harper. Perhaps his word game had been more than a private victory over Tuiloch.

He longed to be with Ainsy now, holding her against him. But in her room it wouldn't be as easy to do what must be done tonight. (Damn that harper and his music! Did he never sleep?) He couldn't chance waking her as he left the room and then trying to explain what he was about. For he'd go naked, ready to take wolfshape as soon as the instrument was destroyed. Wolfshape, or that other he'd worn attacking the brigands. But until the harper slept, it didn't matter where Kern stayed. With the music playing, Tuiloch had his power ready at hand. He could call up the feragh at a moment's notice and Kern's chance would be gone before he made his move.

The feragh. As he thought of the creature, it seemed to Kern that he could hear it moving outside in the snow, could smell the beast's strong reek in his nostrils. He half rose from his straw pallet and—

The music changed. Now it bound him where he lay. Tendrils of sound writhed through his body, binding it with sinewy webs that he no longer had the will to fight. A great darkness washed over him, wave upon wave, until all was black and his head slumped back into the hay.

Senseless he lay while, in the inn yard, a figure stepped from the inn, drawn out of doors by the same power that laid Kern low. There was a blur of silver motion and the figure was flung high in the air like a rag doll. Blood sprayed the white snow, dark and colorless in the moonlight. The figure remained where it had fallen, a limp sprawl of limbs and torso. The harping stopped and the feragh faded. Silence replaced sound and lay over the inn yard like a finely woven pall.

Tenth...

Kern awoke to find someone half lifting him from his straw pallet. He blinked his eyes, trying to clear his head. His thoughts were befuddled and his reaction time was slowed, as though he'd spent the whole night drinking and woke now with the grandfather of all hangovers. The morning light filtering through the barn windows was bright to his eyes. He knew there were people around him, but their faces spun in his vision and he couldn't focus on any of them long enough to make out who they were. The scent of fear was strong in his nostrils, but it wasn't his own.

Motion drew his gaze and suddenly his head cleared. He saw that it was Wat who held him. He raised a hand to push Wat from him, but his arm moved like it was made of lead and the big man only tightened his grip. What had caught his eye was Ainsy moving closer. She'd taken a half step forward, then paused. Her eyes were red from crying.

"You will see that I speak the truth," Tuiloch said, "if

there even be need of further proof."

Kern ignored the harper. Why was everybody staring at him? He tried to fathom the expressions on their faces. Ainsy . . . Wat's face looming over him. Dangerous lights flickered in his eyes that so transformed the big man's usual easygoing expression, Kern hardly recognized him. There was Fion, hard-faced and cold. Tomtim standing well back, one hand on the hilt of the long tinker blade he wore at his belt.

"What . . . what's going on?" Kern managed. His throat felt fuzzy and dry.

"Come see your handiwork," Tuiloch said, "then ask that question again."

"Come see . . . ?"

Kern shook his head, trying to make sense out of what seemed like madness. Something was terribly wrong. Yesterday these people had been his friends. Today they watched him with strangers' eyes. Yesterday he'd been working side by side with Tolly and Wat, and now . . . Kern's blood went cold. Where was Tolly?

Before he could frame the question, Wat hauled him to his feet and shoved him, none too gently, out of the barn, keeping a firm grip on his arm all the while. The white light outside stung Kern's eyes. There was a smell in the air, familiar, sharp, and acrid. And then his eyes adjusted to the glare and he need ask his question no more. He saw what was left of Tolly. The boy had been ravaged by some beast. Half his face was gone. Blood soaked his nightshirt and splattered the snow, dark and red against the white. Kern turned, his stomach giving a lurch.

"Let him go," Tuiloch told Wat. He pulled his harp from his shoulder, settling the straps so that the instrument hung against his chest, and drew a chord from it. "I can control him with a harpspell."

Wat gave Kern another shove and he went sprawling in the snow, his face inches from the perimeter of the terrible stain.

"Sweet stars above!" he cried, turning. "You don't think I—"

"Who else . . . werewolf?"

There. He was named. Numbly, Kern shook his head. A shapechanger he might be, but this boy had been his friend. Did only he hear the gloating in the harper's voice? Did only he see the gleam of pleasure in the dark man's eyes? Tuiloch spoke so glibly of harpspells. Did none of them understand what that meant?

"Please," he said. "Believe me. . . ."

He saw the longknife at the harper's belt now, silver blade against black leather. Tuiloch grinned mockingly, and Kern tore his gaze away to look at the others.

"Ainsy, I. . . ."

"Your hands," she said. Her voice was hollow, her features twisted with anger and grief. "As Arn is our witness, look at your hands."

He did. They were red with dried blood. Tolly's blood. Again he shook his head.

"No! No! This is a lie! I would never have harmed him. He was my friend!"

But he read the look in her eyes and knew that he was already judged. The evidence was plain before them. Whatever he said meant nothing now.

"Your kind have no friends," Tuiloch said.

Tomtim took a step forward. The hand that fingered his tinker blade trembled.

"I guessed what you were," he said bitterly. "That night you rescued me from the brigands. I thought, He helped me. He means me and mine no harm. I know there is magic abroad in the world still, for I've seen enough of it in my years of road wending. I know there is good amid the evil. So I trusted you. I said nothing. Even when Yan Buther was slain, I thought, It was not him. He would not do such a thing. Fool that I was, I trusted you. See how you've repaid me?"

"No! I. . . ."

Again he looked from face to face and knew it was useless to protest. The verdict had been reached and he stood condemned by his own apparent acts. In their place, would he have listened? Tuiloch's magic was strong and Kern could sense the harper's subtle manipulation of their emotions. It needed but a chord—Kern knew too well!—and they would mold to the harper's will. And with Tolly lying dead at their feet, the boy's blood on Kern's hands . . . what could they think but that he'd slain the boy?

"Let us be done with this charade," Fion said. (She who'd feared Ainsy's broken heart. What did she think of him now? It was too clear in her eyes, in her stance.) "He chokes on his own lies. Do what you must, harper."

So easily they accept Tuiloch's magic as benevolent, while he. . . . Kern cut the thought off. He was a shapechanger, nothing more. Alien. Despised. No matter that tears for the slain youth ran hotly down his cheeks. He was the killer. Tuiloch need not work hard to convince them of his evil. He was already condemned by legend and the fear in their hearts. Slowly he stumbled to his feet and turned to face them. Tuiloch grinned, wider than ever, and Kern realized how the harper perceived this moment. The wolf at bay, the hunters gathered for the kill.

It's not my fault, he told himself, but knew different. He should never have stayed. If he'd gone once his wounds were healed, both Tolly and Yan Buther would still be alive. But was it too much to seek peace? Aye, he thought with grim self-pity. Too much for a shapechanger to expect.

He saw Tuiloch's fingers curl about his harpstrings. A last time he looked to Ainsy, but she turned her face from him. The first notes rang across the inn yard, knifed through the silence broken only by Kern's harsh breathing. Then he felt the change coming over him and knew what Tuiloch meant to do. The harper would show them his wolfshape as final proof. And then. . . . He'd have a chance! Would Tuiloch have time to raise the feragh before Kern escaped? Would he even dare to, with the others watching? For then he must slay them all, would he not?

Kern's shoulders hunched and his limbs began to change. He tore at his shirt. He couldn't be trapped in clothing when the wolfshape was upon him. He needed freedom from its restrictions. Buttons popped and he had the shirt open. He was dropping forward onto his forepaws, the shirt hanging loose about him. The boots fell from paws never meant to wear footgear. He wriggled out of his trousers. He saw Tuiloch laughing. Only the harper would find humor in a situation such as this. He saw the faces of the others and they were as still as though their features had been simply painted on. This was the final proof for them.

He readied himself to spring at the harper's throat, then hesitated at the last moment. What good would slaying Tuiloch do now? Ainsy and the others—they'd simply think he'd killed their protector. Better to flee, to return again. Better to somehow clear himself of the murders. People would love him no better, for he'd still be what he was, but they would at least know Tuiloch for what he was.

The thought process took but a fraction of a second. One moment he crouched, muscles bunched to spring, the next he was off, around the barn, the crisp snow under his paws, the shirt flapping about him. He took the time to roll against a bush and tear it from him before running on, unencumbered. And unpursued.

He paused to look back, nostrils sifting the wind. Why was he allowed to escape? Was the feragh waiting to ambush him out of sight of the inn? Had they gathered the neighboring farmers and were they waiting with silver weapons? But the wind came from before him and carried only the smells of snow and forest. Confusion reared in his mind. Why was he not pursued? Then common sense prevailed. What did it matter? He was escaping. That was what was important. He could puzzle over the why's when he was safe.

Turning, he bolted for the woods, conscious of the trail he left behind him in the snow, but simultaneously aware that only the feragh would have the stamina to follow and bring him down. Just so long as Tuiloch held the creature in check—whatever his reasons. . . .

Kern ran on.

Shock held the inn folk in stasis as Kern made his escape. For long moments they stood and stared at his discarded clothing, trying to come to grips with the metamorphosis they had just witnessed. Man to wolf. It was one thing to talk of it, but another to see the change take place before their eyes. So they stood, white-faced and silent, the wind chill on their cheeks, each caught up with the nightmare visions that rode his or her thoughts. Then Fion moved.

"He's getting away!" she cried.

She took a few steps in the direction Kern had taken, then stopped, realizing the futility of her pursuit. The wolf would be long gone by now, vanished in the woods. She whirled to face the harper.

"You let him go!"

Tuiloch shrugged, still plucking idly at his harpstrings.

"So I did. No matter. He'll not escape us. I'll go out after him—once I've breakfasted."

Fion shivered. "Breakfasted? But—" She looked from the harper to Tolly's body and tasted bile. "How can you even think of eating?"

"I am hungry."

The harping grew stronger and strange. Where first it had seemed to play a simple melody, now discordances rang in its music. Fion's thoughts became fuzzy and disordered. There was something she was trying to remember. . . .

Tuiloch smiled. He turned to Ainsy and, while he kept up the music with one hand, cupped her chin with the other. Ainsy regarded him blankly. Still smiling, Tuiloch brushed her lips with his own. She shuddered, but did not draw away.

"Are you mine?" the harper asked, pulling a stronger chord from his instrument.

Ainsy nodded, and this time when the harper kissed her, she did not recoil. Rather, she leaned against him. Tuiloch left off his harping then and faced the others.

"You, half-wit," he told Wat. "Get rid of that." He pointed to the corpse. "And you, old man. Give him a hand. Fion." He spoke her name like a caress and she trembled. "Fix us some breakfast, like a good girl."

He swung his harp to his back and made for the inn, one arm around Ainsy, fondling her breast.

"I have yet to see your room," he said as they reached the inn door. "I picture it as warm and inviting, with dried wildflowers and pretty ornaments. Am I right?"

Without a will of her own, Ainsy could only nod. Her mind was empty, holding only what the harper wished it to hold. Tuiloch paused to look back across the inn yard. Then laughing, he followed her to her room.

Fion watched them go. She knew she should be making breakfast, but something was troubling her. She glanced at Wat and Tomtim, who were dragging Tolly's body unceremoniously toward the river, hauling their burden as though it were no more than a load of wood. The corpse was stiff and left a swath in the snow behind it, bordered on either side by the men's footprints. Lips pursed, Fion followed their progress until the barn blocked her view. She felt nothing. She wasn't aware that she should feel anything. But still something nagged at the back of her mind.

Stram crept from the barn where he'd been hiding and distracted her. The dog came to her on its belly, tail between its legs and whining.

"What's the matter with you?" she asked, and knelt to ruffle the hair around its ears.

Then, regarding the dog, she remembered something. Of course Stram was frightened! There had been a creature . . . something terrible. A man that could change into a wolf. Fear chilled her, sharp and sudden. She saw again the change, man becoming wolf, the red fur and the dangerous lights in its eyes. Then she relaxed. Tuiloch would protect them from it. He'd promised to hunt it down after breakfast. Breakfast! How could he go hunting if she didn't get it ready?

She hurried to the kitchen. From the window, she could see Wat and Tomtim returning, their hands empty, burden gone. As they went about their chores, she finished mixing her batter and poured it into the frying pan. The batter sizzled and the pleasant smell of cornmeal pancakes filled the kitchen. Laughter came from Ainsy's room and she smiled. Ainsy had finally found her man. And what a man! Lean and handsome, mage and harper. Not like that other one: Kern of the lies and terrible secrets.

Fion froze. Kern. His face was in her mind, superimposed over the image of a wolf's head. Lady Arn above! How could she have forgotten? Numbly she rose from the hearth and went to the window. The snow was still red where Tolly's body had lain. She squeezed her eyes shut, massaging her temples with trembling fingers. Kern had killed him. Butchered him. There. In the inn yard.

She heard laughter again, floating down the hall from Ainsy's room and it all came back to her. The harper waking them. Finding Tolly slain. Tuiloch leading them into the barn where Kern lay, Tolly's blood dried on Kern's hands. A werewolf's hands. . . .

Slowly she turned from the window to stare down the hall. Tuiloch and Ainsy. They were making love in Ainsy's room and Tolly not half a day dead. How could they? How had *she* forgotten? What could possibly have come over her?

The answer came from a small voice that whispered in the back of her mind. Bespelled. Tuiloch had ensorcelled them. To forget. To. . . . Revulsion gripped her and her knees began to tremble. She sank to the floor, arms hugging her stomach, eyes flooding with tears. Tolly was dead. She remembered Tuiloch's harping with new ears, heard the evil in it, the discordance that sapped the will and laid his own in its place. Tolly was dead and slain not by Kern—as wolf or man—but by magic. Harpmagic. Why? Blessed Arn, why?

The byplay last night, between Kern and the harper, returned to her. Tuiloch's courting Ainsy and Ainsy's blind acceptance of him then and now . . . now. . . . She lifted tear-blind eyes to the hallway and recoiled. Tuiloch stood there, clad only in his black trousers, arms folded across his naked upper torso.

"You!" she spat, and clawed her way to her feet. *"You* killed Tolly!"

She scrabbled on the counter for the bread knife, but Tuiloch crossed the room in swift, long strides and slapped it from her hand. She leaped at him with clenched fists and he backhanded her across the face, knocking her to the floor. Before she could rise, he was upon her, his weight bearing her down. The slender fingers grasped her neck, and lifting her head, he cracked it against the floor. Once. Twice.

Pain exploded in her head. His fingers sought the carotid arteries in her neck and, finding them, squeezed, cutting off the flow of blood to her head. Just before she lost consciousness, he relented, his grip loosening. His face was inches from her own. Her vision spun. All she could see were the two soulless pale grey orbs that were his eyes. They pierced her, pinning her as hypnotically as a snake might a hare.

"I must stop underestimating you valley folk," he said.

Fion's mind was a roar of pain and brittle sound, but each word the harper spoke dropped into that turbulence as sharp and clear as though in a deadly silence.

"Now listen," he added, "and perhaps you will still live. Spoil my game, and I'll kill you as easily as I did your stableboy. But if you do as you're told. . . ."

He worked two levels. Vocally, he threatened, but Fion didn't cow easily. His eyes were like the harpmagic and she could feel them leech at her will, drawing her under his power. Grimly she fought him. The eyes were like a morass, swallowing her into them, but she concentrated on Tolly, on what the harper had done to him, and found the strength to hold her own. Still the harper was powerful. And, did she escape the command of his magic, there were still his fingers around her throat. For all his slender frame, he had strength enough to kill her. She needed to buy herself time.

So, slowly, she let him think that he won. She fought still, but with an ever-lessening will, so that when the final acquiescence came, it appeared natural. Inevitable. Tuiloch watched her for long moments, then loosened his grip upon her throat. He trailed his fingers across her face, along cheek and chin, down to her breasts, his gaze fixed on hers all the while, weighing her reactions. With the greatest effort of will, Fion kept her features bland.

At last, Tuiloch smiled and, standing, helped her to her feet.

"Give us a kiss," he said.

Dutifully, she did, though inwardly she recoiled with revulsion. Tuiloch's smile grew wider.

"Your corn cakes are burning," he said.

As she turned to see to them, she heard him leave. She pulled the pan from the hearthstone, then sank to her knees. Her chest was constricted with emotion, her throat ached with the need to weep. But she knew she could not let one tear fall. To be helpless. . . . She shook her head, forcing hatred to take the place of her frustration and fear. The movement sent a new wave of dizziness through her. She had won only a battle—as small a victory as Kern's last night. The war was still to come. Her enemy held all the trumps. She had only herself. . . .

Kern. She went back to the confrontation in the inn yard. She was convinced now of Kern's innocence. Only what had she seen there? Man to wolf. More of Tuiloch's lies? An illusion? She wiped her nose on the sleeve of her dress and returned to the window. The red snow brought another lump to her throat. But there beside it lay Kern's trousers and boots. So the change had been real.

Had Tuiloch keyed it, or was Kern simply a man, trapped now in the shape of a wolf? If she could find him, would she be dealing with a man or a beast? She remembered his wounds and how swiftly they had healed, the lightness of his step, the wariness about him, the strength for a man so small.

Looking past the barn to the forest beyond, she wondered as well: how could she even hope to find him out there? He could be anywhere. Leagues from here, if he had any sense. Only would he desert them? She weighed his gentle manner and his love for Ainsy against their treatment of him this morning. What had she seen in his eyes as they'd all accused him? Fear? Surely. But resignation as well. Perhaps he had been concealing his shapechanger's ability for fear of those very reactions. That would make it both easier and more difficult. Easier, for she would be dealing with a man who could control his shape. But if he was a shapechanger, this would not be the first time that he'd been driven away from somewhere. With what he knew they thought of him, how could he even hope for reconciliation?

Fion sighed. She could only try. It would be difficult to search for him, for she had Tuiloch to worry about as well. He would not let her go out wandering the countryside, looking for help. And this afternoon. . . . He meant to hunt Kern.

It was all too much for her. Only her hatred for Tuiloch kept her from utter despair. It settled in her, cold and hard. Unyielding. She would try to find allies. If that didn't work, she would try alone. The harp seemed the key. Music. He had power without it—her bruised neck bore witness to that—but not so much as with the harp. With the instrument destroyed. . . . She shook her head. It was too early to make plans.

Returning to the hearth, she dumped the remains of the spoiled cakes into the fire and began the meal anew. When it was ready, she called the others to the table, composing her features into the same bland expressions that they wore.

It tore at her heart to see them so. Especially Ainsy, who watched the harper with the eyes of a lovesick cow. How she longed to ram the bread knife down his throat.

But he was watching her, more so than he watched the others, or so it seemed to her in her guilt. Seething inwardly, she played her part, fawning over him, hanging on to his every word like the rest did. And if Tuiloch suspected her, he made no outward show of it.

Eleventh...

At first Kern simply fled.

He ducked under low branches, where the snow was thinner and the going easier, pacing himself at a mile-eating gait. But as the rush of adrenaline slowed and the deep silence of the snow-bound woods permeated his being, he slowed down, then stopped altogether. It seemed like madness to push himself when the need wasn't immediate.

He kept constant guard as he rested, testing the wind, ears cocked for the faintest sound. The snow was not deep, here between the trees, but deep enough to muffle a footfall. Yet for all he listened and watched and smelled, he found no hint of his enemy. Only then, assured that he was indeed alone with only the forest and snow for company, did he will his manshape to him.

Naked he stood in the snow, but he could have shouted with relief. When the harp had sounded and put his wolf-shape on him, he'd been afraid that the spell was to bind him to this shape forever. A curse his gift might seem at times, but to be trapped always in one shape—that was indeed a greater curse.

Returning to lupine form, he lay down in the snow. His thick red fur kept the chill from him while he replayed the morning's events in his mind. He tried not to think of Tolly, or the expressions of the inn folk as they encircled him, but his thoughts returned to those images time and again. The accusing stares. The hatred and fear that was all the more unbearable coming from those he'd counted as friends. And yet. . . . Having seen what they had seen, without knowing what he knew, what else could they think but that he'd turned on them?

He cradled his muzzle on crossed forepaws, breath wafting from his snout, and stared into the forest. He'd feared the time when Ainsy and the others would know him for what he was, but had never imagined it would come as it had. Tolly. Just sixteen and full of life, reduced to nothing more than a bundle of bloodied clothes and torn flesh. The image was burned into his mind, there for all time. A howl ached in his throat, trembling for release. But he was hunted again and such a cry, no matter how strong his need for it, would only lead the hunter to him.

The hunter. Tuiloch. The harper. Kern snarled, thinking of him. What drove Tuiloch to such lengths? A spoiled hunt? That and no more? Why this need to discredit him as well? Was his elimination not enough?

There were no simple answers. He had no answers at all.

He lay a long while, brooding and turning the events over in his mind. He knew that he wasted precious time. Soon enough Tuiloch would be on his trail. Soon enough he would loose the feragh and finish what was begun those weeks ago on the cliff overlooking the Tattershall. Kern should be fleeing now, putting as much distance between himself and them as he could. But something held him where he was, bound him to this spot, and Kern knew it for what it was, as surely as he knew his own name.

It was his love for Ainsy that kept him here.

She might hate him for what she thought he'd done, might fear him and never wish to see him again, unless he be dead and his head carried before the hunters on a spear. All that might well be true—was true. There was no need for pretense with himself. No hope of reconciliation lay between them. But that changed nothing. Not the way he felt for her, or his memories of her; nor did it ease the ache inside.

Sighing, he rose and, shaking the snow from his fur, trotted off through the woods. Not west, deeper into the forest and to safety, but east, to the inn and what he'd fled. He would go cautiously, with greater care than he'd ever exercised before. Even if he must flee again, he would look on her once more. If only from a distance.

The way back took him twice as long, for the speed that came from charged adrenal glands was no longer upon him. He had, as well, his own nervous fears to contend with. What if he met Tuiloch upon the way? What if, seeing Ainsy, he could not leave? Was it better to risk all for this parting view, or flee as he knew he should?

It began to snow again and a goodly part of his nervousness fell away with it. The snow would hide both his trails, the old and the new. It fell thick and fast, great big flakes that hung from his fur, streaking it white. By the time he reached the orchard near the inn, it fell so hard that it was difficult to see for more than a few yards in any direction. He paused there, checking his surroundings not so much with scent and sound—for the snow dampened them—as with a sixth sense that he'd inherited from his wild brothers. At last he bounded forward, guard hairs hackling with tension.

He circled the back of the inn, scouting for danger, then made his way to the kitchen window. It was too high for him to reach in wolfshape, even standing on his hind legs, so he willed himself into his manshape. He shivered as the winds blew snow against his naked limbs. He stared at the smoky glass, hesitating still, afraid not so much of what he'd see as how he'd react to it. Fingers balanced against the inn's wall, he leaned forward to peer around the window jamb.

For long moments he couldn't even breathe. As he stared inside, a bitterness arose to wash over him. Fool! He was a fool! Thrice-damned and stupid as a newborn pup.

He pulled his head from the window and pressed his

cheek weakly against the wall. A fool, yes. For what had he expected? That they would mourn his going? That they would see through the lie and know that he had nothing to do with Tolly's death? Sweet stars above! They didn't even mourn the stableboy who'd been their friend.

Hot tears started in his eyes, but his sorrow mingled inside with a growing anger. He looked again, ready now for what he would see. They sat around the kitchen table, talking and smiling, tea steaming in mugs before them. Ainsy leaning close to the harper. Even Fion was fawning over him. Wat and Tomtim nodding their heads as Tuiloch spoke, grinning at some joke.

He has ensorcelled them, Kern thought. He has them bound to his will. Fion was closest to the window and to her he reached out with his lupine senses, seeking the spell that had to be there, but was not. That essence of magic, which was intuitable to a creature of magic such as Kern, was not present. Kern shook his head. How could they *not* be ensorcelled? Does it all mean so little to them? Never mind his own seeming betrayal. What of the deaths of their friend and the farmer? Could they not smell the stench of lies that cloaked Tuiloch as surely as though they were of the brightest cloth and hung from his shoulders?

The sorrow in him died and the anger rose strong. Deep in his man chest a wolf growl rumbled—low, hardly audible. He longed to smash the window and leap in among them, to attack Tuiloch where he sat so complacently, to take the lot of them by the throat and shake some sense into them. But what use was it? Tuiloch was what he was—powerful and no match for Kern. And the others . . . it seemed that they had made their choice.

He began to turn away when he sensed he was no longer alone. He ducked as something swiped the air where he'd been. Glass shattered above him, showering him. The strong reek of the feragh was all around him. How could he not have sensed its approach? Heard it? Smelled the damn creature? Kern rolled along the wall and bolted, legs pumping as he crossed the inn yard and made for the river. The drifting snow dragged at his legs, slowing him. He stole a glance behind. The feragh followed at its lumbering silent gait. The snow didn't appear to touch its fur or impede its progress. When Kern reached the far side of the inn yard, he paused to take his wolfshape, then ran once more.

Now he made better time, bounding over the snow, broad paws like snowshoes, wolf muscles propelling him through the deeper drifts. As he ran, he waited expectantly for the harpmusic, knowing that when it came he would lose his momentum as it sapped his will. As it had before. But till that moment, he'd give it his best.

If he should win free this time, he knew what he must do. Flee until he placed the mountains between him and the harper's magic. His reason for besting the harper was gone. Now he sought only his own life and freedom.

Ainsy and the others had made their own choice. He should strive to aid them when they sided willingly with his enemy? Freely, without the harpmagic to charm them? A fool he might be at times, but not utterly blind.

By the time he reached the river he'd gained a good lead on the feragh. The surface of the river wasn't deeply frozen yet—just the first few inches, but that would be enough to bear his weight. He paused when he saw the jagged hole near the shore—black and stark against the white snow. Tolly, he thought, sensing instinctively what had become of the stableboy's corpse. Again anger reddened his sight and this time he loosed the howl that demanded release. It tore rawly from his throat, relaxing some of the tension that gripped his chest.

He crossed the river and headed through the frozen marshes. The snow still fell thick and steady. He raised a cloud of fluff and seeds as he tore through a bulrush thicket, but the heavy snow kept it from floating far. The feragh stayed behind him, following at a steady pace. The distance between them lengthened, but Kern knew the creature would stay on his trail. It was an unnatural thing, born of magic, inexorable, tireless. As long as Tuiloch's will kept it on Kern's trail, there it would stay, until the moment came when Kern could run no more. Yet unless Tuiloch used the harping spell again, that time was still distant. Kern was in strong form. His wounds no longer troubled him. And though he fled for his life, he took a certain delight in how the white ground sped by underfoot, in the whip of the snow against his face and the roll of his muscles as they propelled him onward.

I will give you a run, he thought. One you will not soon forget.

The snow hid all sight of his pursuit, killed scent, muffled sound. But Kern knew the feragh still came. He could sense the raw power of it behind him, its unnatural presence. He thought again of what he'd seen at the Tinker and fled more quickly—not so much from fear as from the horror he felt inside at what he'd seen.

Ainsy's features swam in his mind and he cried to her: How could you? Then he stifled the wash of sorrow. He'd be better off burying his memories of her along with those of Tera and his parents. There was nothing for him at the Tinker now. And ahead? The future? What lay for him there? He tried to still the flow of his thoughts, but they rose up to torment him all the same. Peace was lost again. The security of a home. The love of a woman who loved him. All this was denied him anew.

You are one of the wild, he told himself. It is better this way. Better than living a lie. Better that it should happen now, than a year from now. Than ten years from now. Forget, he thought fiercely. Forget. To brood brings only torment. The advice was good, but the memories were still too fresh, the hurts too raw. But for all the self-pity that flooded him, still he fled on. And behind, the feragh maintained its relentless pursuit.

Twelfth...

When the window smashed, Fion dropped her tea mug with a clatter, then shot a glance at Tuiloch. Was she supposed to be so bound to his will that she shouldn't have noticed such a thing? She need not have worried. The others at the table looked as startled as she did, all save the harper. He merely smiled.

"Arn above!" Ainsy cried.

She leaped to her feet, staring at the window. There was a flash of a silver paw the size of a bear's amid the jagged smoky glass that was gone so quickly that no one was sure of what they'd seen.

"Sit," Tuiloch said, and put his hand on her arm. "It is only the wolf, returned to try us again. But you needn't be afraid. I have awoken a guardian to patrol the inn yard. The wolf will not get by our protector."

Ainsy sat, soothed by the harper's words. Shock and fear left her features and they smoothed into blandness once more.

Fion hardly noticed her or any of them. She could have

shouted for joy. Kern had returned! He hadn't fled, though she would not have blamed him if he had. Tuiloch's talk of a guardian worried her, but at least now she had something to aim for. If she could reach Kern and if between them they could come up with a way to overcome the harper. . . .

She composed her features. She would wait until tonight, then go look for him. The after-image of the white paw at the window flashed in her mind. She tried not to think of what fell creature Tuiloch might have set to be their guardian. So long as she could get by it and to Kern. . . . Her pulse sounded a drumming rhythm in her chest and she hoped it wasn't as loud as it sounded to her. But Tuiloch was ignoring her: He directed Tomtim and Wat to the window and had them nail up boards to shut out the storm.

Fion glanced at Ainsy, wishing there was some way she could get through to her. Surely if she knew the truth, she'd help. But Tuiloch held her on too tight a rein. And perhaps it was better that she acted on her own. Tuiloch watched Ainsy too closely. Should she rebel as Fion did, could she keep it from him?

As for the others. . . . She wasn't sure she could depend on Wat. His heart was in the right place and he had strength in his limbs, but to ask him for cunning. . . . She could not risk it. And as for Tomtim, the tinker was old and still recovering from his ordeal with the brigands. He was her best chance, only how to get to him? How to break Tuiloch's hold?

Fion sighed inwardly. No, she'd have to do it on her own. Tonight, when it was dark and Tuiloch was ensconced with Ainsy in her bedroom. Fion's features hardened at the thought of that, but what could she do? Hateful as it was, at least it would keep Tuiloch occupied and give her a chance to steal away. Ainsy would recover from the abuse of her body. She would not recover from death.

"You draw the wolf," Tuiloch was saying to Ainsy, "as surely as apple blossoms draw bees. He has escaped us this time, but he will return. Again and again—until we slay him. Would you like to deal the killing blow when we do catch him?"

Something glittered hard and bright in Ainsy's eyes as she nodded.

"Willingly," she said.

But the word came not so much from her as from Tuiloch's mind.

Fion looked away. If they survived, she prayed that Ainsy would remember none of this. To see her like this, she who was always so strong-minded and self-willed. . . . Images of the morning returned to haunt her: Tolly sprawled in the snow, lifeless; Kern changing from man into wolf and fleeing; Ainsy giving herself to Tuiloch; and the harper, his eyes dark with emotion as he worked his will on them all. How could so much evil be in one man? She watched him from under hooded eyelids, dropping her gaze when he glanced at her. He must *not* suspect, she thought. Lifting her gaze, she leaned across the table and smiled at him.

"Tell us another tale," she said.

Tuiloch's eyebrows lifted. There was a strange expression in his eyes and again Fion heard the thunder of her own heartbeat. But he only tapped the rim of his mug and returned her smile.

"More tea?" he asked.

While she poured him another serving, he closed his eyes.

"This one is from Lyntergn," he said, "and tells of Ilst and the winds of Remen. It seems, a long time ago, there was a shepherd named Ilst. A bold lad he was and given to boasting. . . ."

As nightfall approached, the snow let off and Kern reached the far borders of the marshes. The north winds drove the storm clouds on, and as the light leaked away, the sky overhead grew velvet dark and hung with stars. By the time full night had come, the moon was lifting into the sky and soon the snowswept fields were guttering and bright under her reflective light.

In the distance, Kern could discern the outriding trees of the Gwenwood. The snow-laden branches seemed to beckon him, promising shelter, but he paused at the edge of the marsh to study his backtrail. The indefinable sense that kept him aware of his pursuit was silent and, looking back, he could see nothing, feel nothing. It was as though the feragh had never been on his trail. He stood stiff and still for long moments, perceptions honed to a razor-fine point as he sought his pursuer. Troubled, he trotted a few paces back into the frozen marsh, guard hairs hackled in anticipation. Still nothing.

He could not believe himself free. After all of Tuiloch's subtle machinations, it was too much to expect him to be satisfied with simply driving Kern off. And the feragh, supernatural creature that it was, could not have tired. Had the hunt been called off? And if so, why?

Kern knew he should be taking advantage of this moment. With luck, he could even be out of the valley before Tuiloch called the hunt up again. Kern could hide in the mountains, waiting for another storm, and lose his trail completely in the ensuing snows and wind. Could even harpmagic track him through the winterbound mountains? But go on though he should, he could not shake the feeling that he had missed something of vital importance. If he went on now, it seemed, he went on to his doom.

At length, he set off along his backtrail. He was wearying, but kept doggedly to it, taking time out only to chase down a winter-furred hare to fuel his body for what was to come. The return was easier, for he followed the path he'd broken through the snow earlier. He need not break new ground. Two hours later he came to where the feragh had turned back.

He almost missed it, for he was searching for a trail that a huge beast might make, while the feragh's actual tracks were shallow, as though it walked atop the soft snow, instead of sinking as its weight should have called for. The feragh's musky spoor still hung in the air.

Kern followed its faint tracks, every nerve wound tight with tension. He expected at any moment to see the creature come charging out of a willow thicket or stand of dried rushes. But the night remained still, and though the moon shone brightly, he saw nothing but shadows and snow, heard nothing but the faint click of his claws on the places where the wind had cleared the ice, heard his own breathing and the rasp of the marsh thickets brushing his fur.

He went as far as a small hillock that twisted out of the marsh, high-backed and treed with cedar. In the summer it would be an island, surrounded on all sides by marsh and stagnant water, a secret place for muskrat or beaver to gather. Tonight it was unvisited. Kern started up the rise, then hesitated. The wind came from behind him. His ears and eyes told him that the hillock was devoid of any presence, but his sixth sense whispered a warning. Backtracking, nerves still on edge, he circled the hillock, coming up to it from the northwest.

Now the wind brought a familiar scent to him, but before he could place it, a dark bulk moved among the cedars and stepped out to meet him. Expecting the worst, Kern crouched, a growl rumbling low in his chest. He was poised to attack or flee. Then, as the bulk moved into the moonlit snow, he placed the scent.

A bull moose faced him—a half ton of muscle and bone, seven feet tall, with a palmated antler spread of five feet. Tendrils of frosty breath clouded the air as it snorted. The antlers wove back and forth. Kern began to retreat. If the moose had laid claim to the hillock as its own territory, he had no intention of disputing its rights to it.

But Kern's scent registered in the moose's brain. Instinctive nervousness surfaced. Where there was one wolf, there would be more. It shook its head and the antlers struck the cedar boughs, knocking a spray of snow to the ground. The motion of the falling snow was enough to startle the huge beast. The long legs churned into motion and it lumbered off, forgoing all claim to the hillock and its cedar shelter.

Kern watched until it was out of sight, then moved up the slope, in among the cedars. There he lay with the still-green boughs screening him from wind and stars, upon a mattress of dry red branchlets.

Unbidden, thoughts of Ainsy stole into his mind and refused to be dislodged. It was only three weeks or so that he'd known her, he told himself. Now that time is past and gone. Forget her as she's forgotten you. But etched in his mind was the image of her leaning close to the harper and, for all his vows, a sharp pain stirred in him. He rose restlessly, pacing the narrow confines of the shelter before lying down once more.

Vague premonitions of danger flickered through him. He should be on his way, fleeing while he had the chance. To remain here was the height of folly. But he was weary—his body from the long chase, but more his spirit. Memories of the inn and Ainsy, of what might have been and of what was, darted through him, chasing each other like the jagged edges of a fever dream from which there was no escape.

He lay and brooded, his thoughts spiraling ever more inward. Had the feragh come upon him now, he would never have noticed. Not until the silver claws bit into his flesh and physical pain drew him out of his dark thoughts.

When Tuiloch sensed the feragh's return to the inn yard, he broke off his storytelling in the middle of a phrase. More than harpmagic bound the mythic beast to him. It was an extension of the darkness that had taken root in the harper's soul, long years ago, and now was a fixed aspect of his personality. The feragh gathered shape from harpmagic, but it was truly no more than an extension of Tuiloch's will, a foil against which the harper sharpened the dark thrusts of his power, the one companion that had endured over the years and never turned away from him. It was the nameless son that Tuiloch had never had, as much a child of his spirit as he was of his own mother's womb.

Tuiloch's eyes glittered now as, thought to thought, the feragh communicated the results of its hunt. He nodded to himself when the report was done. The feragh was to have turned its quarry back to the inn for the final reckoning, but the storm and the shaper's own preternatural resources had spirited it beyond the feragh's grasp. It needed Tuiloch's own hand in it now. First to find the shaper, then to drive him back to this place. Yet it must be done with finesse. Simple butchery had never been the harper's way.

"We are all weary," he said suddenly, looking from blank face to blank face around the table. "Surely it is time we were abed?"

Like automatons, the inn folk rose from their seats and made for their rooms, never questioning the early hour or wondering how the tale, which still lay half-told in their minds, ended.

Ignoring their departure, Tuiloch crossed the room to where his harp stood and took the instrument up on his lap. He trailed his fingers along the strings, awaking unconnected sounds rather than a recognizable tune. Then from the disorder a pattern emerged. Tuiloch rode the music with his thoughts, turning them inward. His eyes closed, and though he retained motor control of his body, he seemed to lift out of himself, hovering a few paces above his head.

He studied his body dispassionately, watched the liquid flow of fingers on strings, the slow rise and fall of his chest. Then, smiling, he drifted out of the inn, passing through walls that proved no obstruction to the insubstantiality of his spirit. He hung in the cold air of the inn yard awhile longer, listening to the music play on inside, marking the silver bulk of the feragh where it guarded the inn door. Then he sped eastward, as swift as the moonlight glinting on the snowy fields.

Thirteenth...

Kern's brooding drew him into a black depression that was so deep he no longer recalled the reasons for it. It lay heavy upon him, cloying and still as stagnant air, drawing its strength from half a lifetime of alienation—self-imposed as much as forced on him by others. Oblivious to the world around him, he stared blindly at the crisscross-hatching of the cedar boughs, his eyes dulled to reflect the numbness of his mind, the despair that rode his heart.

Then slowly he drew out of it. Something called to him. The chill night grew icier still, piercing marrow-deep for all the warmth of his thick fur. A hint of music sprayed about him, hanging from every branched cedar leaf. He stiffened with tension. The root of each hair on his body prickled. Turning, he was not surprised to see the harper sitting across from him. The man's features were calm, almost peaceful. Only his eyes burned with the unquenchable flame of his will.

Kern didn't question how Tuiloch had come to be here—never mind that he should be in the inn, miles west, across the frozen marsh and the Penwater, weaving his games of lies and deceit. There was no strength in Kern's limbs as he regarded his enemy. Only a dull acceptance— the legacy of his depression.

The harper hummed under his breath, the sound converting into harp notes as it left his lips. There was no instrument on his lap. The music crept into Kern's mind and the wolfshape fell from him, so that he lay naked in the cedar mulch. Tuiloch ran his fingers through the thick carpet and, as his humming grew louder, shaped a cloak from the dried leaves. He stood and magnanimously laid it over Kern's trembling shoulders before returning to sit cross-legged across from him once more.

"You wear your wolfshape well," the harper said. "It rings so true that when first I hunted you, I never guessed what lay under that russet pelt."

Kern watched him expressionlessly. Under the black cloud of his depression, a spark stirred. He gauged the distance between them, bunched the muscles of his man legs, tensing them to spring at his foe. The cloak he left where it lay, though the touch of the cloth repulsed him. Its magic stung his nostrils—acrid and bitter. There was the smell of the feragh about it and other scents, more foul.

"I should have known, though," Tuiloch continued. "It is not as though you are the first shaper that I have hunted. That you ran as long as you did, fought the harp-spells—it should have told me. But I never guessed until I saw you that night in the Foxfire. I was not expecting it, I suppose." He shrugged eloquently. "But now . . . now I do know; do I not? You may have spoiled my hunt on the ridge; still, in return you have offered me a much better game. At least you did. But now you refuse to play.

"You mean to flee, don't you? To leave it all behind. Is this the first time you have fled in this manner, or the hundredth? Do friends mean nothing to your kind? Not even the little innkeeper with her brown curls and innocent heart? If you flee, what do you think will become of her?"

"She made her choice," Kern said. His voice sounded strange to his ears—harsh and sullen. "They all chose who to side with. Why should I care what becomes of them now?"

But he did care. Still. Even after they had turned against him. They were the ones who had changed, not him.

"You are still responsible for their pain," Tuiloch said.

"Me? I've done nothing!"

"You set me against them."

Kern shook his head, trying to clear away the confusion that threatened to drive him mad. "Whatever you do to them," he said slowly, "is your responsibility. Not mine."

"Oh?"

There was a world of meaning trapped in that one syllable. It hung between them, sharp as a blade's edge, and dropped into the ensuing silence like thunder. Kern closed his eyes and willed his wolfshape back to him. But the harpmusic rose to fill his head with strange discordances and he couldn't concentrate.

"Why?" he demanded. "Why do you hound me? What have I ever done to you? How can you sit there so calmly, yet do what you do?"

Tuiloch nodded his head complacently at the outburst. "I could say that you spoiled my hunt, denied me my kill," he said by way of explanation. "And to me that would be enough. But it goes deeper than that. I would rid the world of your kind—inhuman soulless creatures that you are. So what does that make me? Demon or avenging angel?"

Kern squeezed his eyes shut. "And Ainsy?" he asked. "And the others? Are they my kind as well?"

"Close enough. They are your friends, are they not?"

"Were. *Were!* And only until they knew me for what I am. You saw yourself how quick they were to turn on me. Why hurt them?"

"It amuses me," Tuiloch said. "They say I have no mercy."

"They? I don't understand."

Amusement flickered in the harper's eyes. "I thought by now you would know me," he said.

He was dealing with a madman, Kern realized. But a madman with the power to follow through the obsessions of his derangement. This entire interview had a surreal quality to it that placed it outside the boundaries of rea-

son, putting it in some misty realm of aberrations and fa-
naticism. He understood Tuiloch's hate—at least its results, if not what it stemmed from. He'd dealt with that
before. Only this time, it seemed, flight was not to be allowed him. And the harper—he was driven by some still
deeper motivation that Kern wasn't sure he could even
begin to understand.

Under the pretense of adjusting the cloak on his shoulders, he sidled a few inches closer to the harper and tried
to plan his attack.

"Who are you?" he asked.

Tuiloch looked up into the cedar boughs, a faint smile
on his lips, and Kern gained another few inches.

"Long ago," the harper said, "my name was Yinadral.
Does that name mean anything to you?"

Kern felt his heart stop inside his chest. Yinadral. The
Wolf-slayer. Who in the kingdoms didn't know that
name? No one knew how many true wolves he'd hunted
and slain, but the count of shapechangers numbered
thirty-seven. Or so it was said. The tales that surrounded
his name were many. No one knew his origin, but his ex-
ploits, at least these attributed to him, were told and re-
told in a hundred stories. It was also said that in his mad
quests to slay Kern's kind, he had murdered countless in-
nocents. Parents used his name to frighten their children.
He was something to shiver over at tale-telling times, on
long winter nights when the fire flickered warm in the
hearth and outside the winter howled. Only. . . .

"Yinadral is dead," Kern said. "He died a hundred years ago."

He fought down his initial surge of fear. He's mad, Kern reminded himself. Powerful, yes, but caught up in delusions of grandeur.

Tuiloch shrugged. "They say the last shapechanger died a hundred years ago as well. On the point of a silver-tipped spear. My spear. But you and I, shaper, we know better, do we not? For you are what you are and you are here, and I—I am what I am."

"Yinadral never had a harp."

But Kern wasn't so certain now. He studied the harper surreptitiously. Another pace and he'd chance it. Tuiloch was slender. How much strength was there in those lean arms? Surely, even in manshape, Kern had a chance against him? There was no feragh here to stand between them.

"How do you know what I did or did not have?" Tuiloch asked. "Remember this: a harp may be heard, but not seen." As he spoke, a cascade of sharp notes rang between them. "I never thought it wise to let the tale tellers give away all of my secrets."

The truth hit Kern hard. He looked down at his hands and flexed them, then regarded the harper once more. If it was true—stars above! If it was true, he didn't stand a chance.

"I see you begin to accept what I say." Tuiloch leaned against a tree, head tilted back to expose the white of his throat. "Then you will also accept that my threats concerning the safety of your friends are no empty words either."

Kern stared at the harper's throat. He clenched his fists.

"What do you want with me?" he asked. "Why not kill me now and be done with the game?"

Tuiloch's gaze caught his, deep and penetrating.

"And so spoil it?" Tuiloch asked softly. "No. Return to the inn and perhaps I'll go easy on your friends. I want them to witness your death. Perhaps I will let them spread about the tale that Yinadral has returned. Your kind are in the ascendant again. Last summer I killed a cousin of yours in Jidian. Did you hear of it? By day she was a slim, fair maid, but at night . . . oh, at night.

"She was not like you. She saw her curse tied to the moon and knew no pleasure in it. But still . . . when I gave her a choice, she refused me. So I slew her younger sister, and when that was not enough, when still she denied her fate, the rest of her family died. She fled as best she was able, but I tracked her down."

"You are a butcher."

"Perhaps. But at least I am a successful one. And I kill with propriety. With skill. Unless I hunt one of your wild brothers. They are only beasts and deserve a quick kill. But you . . . your kind. You are somewhere in between. Pain should be yours and torment, before the kill. How else can you pay for the crime of being what you are?

Had I known you for what you are that day on the ridge, I would never have been so . . . vulgar."

Kern stared at him with loathing. "Then come," he said. "Kill me now and be done with it. Kill me, or leave me in peace."

Tuiloch shook his head, smiling cryptically: "No. I think not. Perhaps I grow soft with age, but I think I will leave you to your peace—such as it is. Until our roads cross again. And they will. They always do. But tell me this, shaper. How much peace will you know when you remember the deaths of the inn folk? Deaths you might have averted?"

Kern leaped at him, but there was nothing substantial to grasp. He passed through the harper's sending and struck the trees behind it with a hard thump. Tuiloch laughed.

"Go," he mocked. "Run in the forest. Cross the mountains. Seek your peace."

Then his image faded with a trickle of jarring harp notes and Kern was alone again.

He stared, slack jawed with amazement, at where the harper had been. Shrugging off the cloak that had not vanished with its creator, he tested his shapechanging ability. The transition was swift and true. In wolfshape he padded out of the cedars and made a long circuit of the hillock, every sense stretched to its limit. Nothing. The harper was gone as though he'd never been. Not even a trace of scent remained—and there had been scent. There had been. . . . Had he dreamed the whole encounter?

Kern shook his head slowly back and forth. The memory of it was too real. Then he saw the cloak, lying in the cedar mulch where he'd tossed it. He sank to the ground and stared westward, through the immediate cedars and miles of marsh that separated him from the inn. Tuiloch. Yinadral. Madman or mythic wolf-slayer? Either way the harper had too much power for Kern to have a hope of killing him. His parting taunts echoed mockingly in Kern's heart. He could go then, could he? It would be as easy as that? But fleeing, he left Ainsy and the others in the harper's hands. Kern had no illusion as to how they'd fare.

The instinct for self-preservation warred against his love for the inn folk. But to return did not necessarily mean they'd be saved. He didn't trust Tuiloch for a moment. The harper used the word *perhaps* too often. Could Kern simply leave them to Tuiloch while he himself went free?

They turned against you, a voice whispered in him. They care nothing for you.

But I care for them.

Even if you defeated the harper, the inn folk would still hate you, still seek your death.

There it was. Whether he won or lost, his own fate was sealed. He thrust his muzzle into the mulch, then lifted it to howl at the sky. Through the cedar boughs he could see the moon, riding high. What am I to do? he howled at her. What am I to do?

Arn shone down silently and Kern huddled against the ground. He hadn't expected the moon to answer. What cared she for him? The black despair returned to crowd his thoughts and he could think no more. He sank into it and let the darkness close over him.

In the common room of the Yellow Tinker, Tuiloch returned to his body and laid aside his harp. He bridged his fingers and, spiderlike, flexed and relaxed them while he recalled the details of his recent encounter with the shapechanger. The creature might still flee. It was either a coward, or wiser than most. For when the game was done, there must be none left to tell the tale of it. No one save him, and he would tell it his own way. As he always did.

But. . . . He smiled. He had still another card to play. There remained the dark-haired chambermaid, who even now lay awake in her bed, waiting for him to seek his own slumber. The shaper was closer to the inn than Tuiloch had thought. Not a long journey for a strong woman on skis. Not a long journey at all. It needed only a thought planted and some guidance.

Still smiling, Tuiloch picked up his harp once more.

Fourteenth...

Does he never sleep?

Fion stared at her darkened ceiling, listening to the eerie sounds of Tuiloch's harp echoing through the inn. She'd waited for what seemed like hours, hearing the music, digging her nails into the palms of her hands, face pressed against her pillows. It was a discordant repetition of notes that grated on her ears. At one point she thought that he must have fallen asleep and only his fingers played on, but she didn't have the courage to look. So she lay awake, trembling with the need to act, but bound to her room as surely as though imprisoned.

When silence finally came, she was drowsing. It jarred her awake, that sudden absence of sound. She sat up in her bed, ears cocked. The quiet dragged into long moments. Then, just as she was about to rise and get dressed, the music started up once more.

This time it was a sparse melody, slow and stately, with a haunting repeat that stuck in her mind. When the harping stopped a second time, she still heard the music and realized that she was humming it herself. She bit at her lip and moved from the bed to press her ear to the door: She could hear Tuiloch moving in the common room, then the *tap-tap* of his boots as he moved down the hall to Ainsy's room. When she heard the door click shut behind him, she wiped sweaty hands on her nightgown. Removing it, she tossed it onto the bed and began to dress.

Soon she stood, bundled in woolen trousers and sweater, with a cloak thrown over and fur-lined boots on her feet. She returned to the door to listen, put her hand to the handle, then thought better of it. Crossing the room, she eased her window open and peered outside. The snow had long since stopped and the moonlight was bright on the white fields. She listened for Tuiloch and tried to spy out the guardian he'd mentioned earlier. In her head, she could still hear the harper's last tune.

She frowned at the music. For all that she tried to think of something else, it stuck in her head. Looking left and right, she could see no sign of Tuiloch's guard. Briefly she wondered what shape it might take, then put that thought from her mind as well before she lost all courage. Drawing a deep breath, she clambered out the window and dropped to the snow. Again she froze, eyes scanning the shadows that huddled around the inn, ears straining for a telltale sound that she was not alone. Nothing. So far so good. Easing the window shut behind her, she made her way alongside the inn's stone wall.

She reached the barn without being discovered and allowed herself a short rest. Her legs quivered—though more from tension than from the cold. With her breath wreathing her face, she stole into the barn, took down her skis, and hurried outside again. She was just turning the corner of the barn, skis hugged against her chest, when she caught movement out of the corner of her eye. She pressed against the side of the barn, trying to merge with the long beams of its logs, and stared back at the inn.

A silvery shape moved in the shadows there. Fion's breath caught in her throat as she took in its size. Arn, she prayed. Don't let that thing find me. She remembered again the flash of a huge paw at the kitchen window and unsuccessfully tried to suppress a shudder. What was she doing out here? It was madness. In a moment that creature would sense her and she'd end up like Tolly, torn apart and lifeless in the snow. Would Tuiloch blame her death on Kern as well? Probably.

The Moon Lady seemed to hear her prayers tonight, for the beast moved on, oblivious to her presence. Slowly, she regained her courage. Pushing herself weakly away from the barn wall, she went on, not stopping until she'd placed the building between her and the inn. There she dropped the skis on the snow and, stepping into them, bent down to fasten them to her boots.

Again movement caught her eye and again she froze. A shadow had detached itself from the bulk of the barn and was sidling toward her. Not large enough to be Tuiloch's monster, her reason told her fear. Then what . . . ?

The breath she'd been holding slowly went out. She held out her hand and Stram edged forward on his belly, tail tucked between his legs. He quivered when she touched him and a tiny whine escaped.

"Whisht," she whispered. "Not a sound, Stram, my love."

She stroked him steadily, easing her own tension as much as the dog's. She found herself humming the harper's tune once more and angrily cast it from her mind. But no sooner was she standing, slipping the loops of her poles onto her wrists, than it was back, sidling through her thoughts.

Damn that harper! If all he'd done wasn't enough, now she had his bloody music stuck in her head. She had to stop thinking of him. The better part of the night was already gone and she'd yet to set out. Kern could be anywhere. Nearby, watching her now, or miles away. Suddenly the enormity of her task sank in. Almost she turned back, there and then, but a thought rose unbidden in her. The marshes. He'll have gone into the marshes.

She didn't stop to think of where the thought had come from, or how she could know. At this point, one direction was as good as another, and she had to get moving before she completely lost her nerve.

"Kern," she murmured to Stram. "We must find Kern."

The dog's ears perked up at the sound of the name.

"Kern," she repeated. "Find Kern."

Stram moved back and forth before her, then took a

few steps in the direction of the marshes, paused, and looked over his shoulder at her. That settled it, she decided. She shuffled forward on her skis. She'd waxed the bottoms recently and soon built up enough momentum to shift into a rolling, skatinglike motion. The tips of her skis kicked up puffs of snow. Her poles sank deeply with each shove she gave them. And Stram ran on ahead.

Soon they reached the slope leading to the river. Fion skimmed down the incline. Desperately, she tried to avert her eyes from the jagged hole in the ice where Wat and Tomtim had disposed of Tolly's body. But it was already too late. She looked away and the image of the hole remained in her mind. Tolly's face was superimposed over it. Hot tears welled up in her eyes and froze on her cheeks.

Grimly she pushed the images away. There would be a time for grief. But now she must concentrate on finding Kern. If she didn't, they could very easily all end up like Tolly, and the harper might go on his way, never having paid for his crimes. So she hurried on, following the dog—though sometimes it seemed that she was leading him more than he leading her.

She kept to the skating motion on the flatter surfaces, climbing the steeper inclines with her skis parallel, horizontal to the slopes. The further into the marshes they got, the more she trusted the stray thought that had sent her there to begin her search. It felt right, and Stram, if he understood her at all, stayed ahead of her as if on

Kern's scent. More quickly than she might have hoped, the distance fell away behind them.

Tuiloch stepped from the inn just as Fion and Stram entered the marshes. The feragh shuffled silently to him and paused at his side.

"The dog's convinced her, if my own harpspell was not enough," he said, ruffling the feragh's silver fur. "What do you think?"

The beast rumbled a low reply and Tuiloch smiled.

"Aye. Soon enough it will be over and we will need to seek a new game to play." He gave the big head a last playful rumple, then turned to reenter the inn.

"Remember," he added, before he closed the door. "Do not harm them. Let them make the inn, though do not make it too easy for them. Now go."

He slapped a silver flank. The door closed with a soft click. For a long moment the feragh stood staring at it with unblinking eyes. Then it returned to prowling the shadows of the inn's eaves, at length hunching down in the snow where it became only one more of many drifts.

Fion found the hillock as though she'd had her route unerringly planned before ever setting out. When she saw it from a distance, she knew immediately that she would find Kern there. She didn't even need Stram's excitement to convince her. With that feeling of success riding high in her, she felt that Tuiloch was already beaten. All she need do was sit down with Kern and work out the details of it.

Then she reached the hillock. She looked up into the dark shadows of the cedars, Stram quiet at her knee, and she wasn't so sure anymore. Would Kern even listen to her? How could she even be sure that he was here? He must be. He had to be! He was. The feeling inside her was too potent.

She bent down to undo her fastenings and, stepping free of the skis, stuck them upright in the snow. She had her back to the hillock and was about to turn when she sensed movement behind her among the cedars. Stram lowered his stomach to the ground, pressing his muzzle into the snow. Kern, Fion thought. It had to be. How would he greet her? Would it be a man she faced or a wolf? An outstretched hand or a grim furred shape leaping for her throat? Stram certainly didn't look like he'd be any help. For long moments she stood frozen where she was, then slowly she turned.

He was waiting for her up the slope, the incline giving him an appearance of height. He had a cloak thrown over his shoulders, but wore nothing else. She shivered to look at his bare legs and feet. His face was in shadow and she had to move toward him before she could judge her welcome. What she saw in his face made her shiver again. She didn't know what she'd expected, but it hadn't been this. The apathy in his eyes, the slack expression of his features, shocked her. Surely he'd burn with anger too? Surely he felt the need to strike back?

"Kern?"

She took a few more steps, stopped, her arms hanging limp at her sides.

"Why have you come?"

He spoke in a monotone, neither friendly nor unwelcoming. It was as though he felt nothing. Whatever she meant to say caught in her throat. His apathy was contagious. She felt a sudden swell of hopelessness wash dully through her.

"Has he sent you," Kern asked, "when his own words failed?"

"What do you mean?"

But already the implication of what he said served to cut through her own dull feeling.

"I mean your precious Tuiloch. Or does he call himself Yinadral at the inn now as well? Yinadral. Wolf-slayer. Protector of the innocent."

He laughed harshly and the sound sent a chill running up Fion's spine.

"Yinadral?" she asked. The name dropped from her lips and she found herself thinking of her dad and his endless supply of tales. She should know that name. It tugged a familiar chord in her. Then she remembered and her mouth shaped an *O*. "You mean Tuiloch is. . . ."

It couldn't be. But Kern was nodding.

"So he says."

Fion tried not to think of what that might mean. Bad enough that they had the harper to deal with, without making him out to be some mythic figure out of legend, something they had no hope of dealing with.

"Kern, please," she said. "Hear me out. I've come here on my own. Stram led me. I know what Tuiloch's done—to us, to you."

She moved closer to him and put out her hand. He backed away from her. There was a feral look in his face now that made her want to draw back herself, but swallowing her fear as best as she was able, she only took another step forward.

"Just listen to me," she said. "For the friendship we had. I know we—*I*'ve treated you unfairly, but. . . . Oh, if you'd just give me a chance."

He looked at her for long moments, unblinking as only a wild animal might. Then shrugging, he turned and retreated into the cedars. Fion glanced at her ski poles, had the sudden desire to take one in among the trees with her, but pushed it aside. She inhaled deeply to steady her nerves, then followed him in.

He sat against a tree, his legs curled under him, cloak wrapped around him. The moonlight stole in through gaps in the boughs above, making shafts of light against the deeper shadows. Stram crept by her and approached Kern, whimpering softly.

"Is it that you've not forsaken me," Kern said to the

dog, "or that your betrayal troubles you and you wish to make amends?" He sighed, ruffled the dog's fur, and looked at Fion. "So speak," he said.

His gaze followed her as she sat down across from him, never leaving her face for a moment.

"I . . . I don't know where to begin."

"Why not where the harper left off?"

"Tuiloch didn't send me! I swear to you, I came on my own, with no one to know except the dog. Why do you keep making it seem otherwise?"

"What else am I to think?" Kern asked. "You made it plain enough this morning who you believed. All of you. And later, when I stole back, I saw you all sitting around the kitchen table—as we'd sat so many times before. I saw you hanging on to his words, like a bunch of puppets. I cast for magic, I cast *you* for magic, to see if he'd ensorcelled you, but there was nothing there!"

"But, Kern—"

He shook his head, cutting her off. "I know what I am—how it fills you with fear and revulsion. It's not hard to understand your siding with . . . with him."

"Please," she said. "You said you'd listen."

"I didn't kill Tolly!"

All apathy was gone from him now. The tendons in his neck stood out as he shouted the words. A vein pulsed at his temple. His eyes burned with anger. Stram backed away with a puzzled whine.

"No matter what you think, it's a lie! I never touched

him!" He held up his hands. "The blood was there, I know, but I didn't put it there!"

"I know," she said quietly.

It took a moment for her words to sink in.

"You . . . you know? Then why . . . ?"

"I didn't know then. We *were* ensorcelled then. The rest still are. I broke free—don't ask me how. Maybe I was just too angry for the spell to take hold. Or too close to Tolly. I only pretended to be the same as the rest. I went along in the hope that I could do something. How or what I don't know. But he has to be stopped. There's only us left."

Slowly Kern's anger seeped away. He recalled that moment when he'd peered into the kitchen, just before the feragh attacked. He'd only checked Fion. None of the others. And if she'd been pretending. . . .

"Ainsy?" he asked.

"She's ensorcelled. I swear it, Kern. She loves you still. It's the harper that speaks through her, not her."

Hope rose in him only to dissolve again. He shook his head.

"It doesn't matter," he said. "I'm still what I am. Magic or not, she'll hate me when she knows what I am."

Fion longed to tell him otherwise, but couldn't lie. There had to be truth between them. She was only just coming to grips with her own feelings about him. Was she accepting what he was or just putting the horror of it aside because she needed his help and there was no one else? No one else who'd even believe, little say help. Arn help them both, she didn't know. She read the anguish in his eyes, but couldn't form the words he needed to ease it. The silence between them intensified.

"What did you mean," she said, needing to say something, "when you said Tuiloch's own words failed?"

Thinking of the harper rekindled the fires in his eyes again.

"He was here, but he wasn't here. It was a sending, or something. I don't know. It *seemed* real. I could see him, smell him. I. . . . He told me it was all a game. That you and the rest were involved only because of me and that whatever harm came to you would be my fault. He gave me a choice: go back to the inn so that he could kill me before you, or allow you all to die.

"I thought . . . I thought you'd all sided with him. Thought there was no magic involved in your decision. I couldn't decide whether to keep on running or go back. I. . . ." His features twisted. "I still can't decide. Why should it be my fault? I did nothing! I am the way I am because I was born this way, but I'm not evil. The first time I killed a man in my wolfshape was when I rescued Tomtim from the brigands. I swear it was the first time! I'm not evil. Why should I be blamed?"

"It . . . it's not your fault," Fion said. "Tuiloch's the one that's evil. We're all equally his victims. All of us."

For long moments Kern said nothing. Then: "I wish I could believe that. I know in my heart that it's true, but if it wasn't for me, Tolly'd still be alive and none of this would have happened."

"You can't blame yourself for Tuiloch's evil."

"No? Tell me, Fion. How do you feel about me? About what I am? Could you still be my friend? Could you still trust me?"

He threw off the cloak and willed the wolfshape to him. Stram whined and Fion drew back in fright, then tried to steady herself as best she could. She stared at the red-furred wolf. Only the eyes were still Kern's. The rest . . . She fought down a shudder and reached across to touch him. The fur on his neck was grizzled. On his head it was softer.

"I . . . I could try," she said.

Suddenly the fur turned to curls and Kern moved back against the tree in manshape, tugging the cloak about him.

"You're very brave," he said softly. "I know that you believe all the tales of my kind, yet you're still willing to make the effort. Was it hard?"

"It was. . . ."

She explored the feeling, pushed beyond the fear to her own inner core, and realized that the friendship they'd known overrode the fear. She shook her head.

"No," she said. "Not as hard as I thought it would be."

"And Ainsy?" Kern asked. "How would she feel, do you think?"

"I don't know. She'd have to work that out for herself. I can't promise anything, Kern. I can't even promise how my own feelings'll go. Perhaps it's only the greater threat of Tuiloch that makes it easy now, and later . . . later it might be harder. I don't like to think that I'm trying to use you, but . . . I don't *know,* Kern."

A bitter smile touched his lips. "Then what's the use? Win or lose, I'd still lose. Even if we defeated Tuiloch, I'd have nothing. I'd still be fleeing. I've been running my whole life, Fion. I always knew it, inside, but I managed to hide it from myself until I came to the Tinker. Then I saw a chance. A home. A woman who loved me. Friends. Now it's all gone."

"You're only thinking of yourself," Fion said. "What about us? We need your help. For the friendship we had. . . ."

"You need my help? Or perhaps my death? Is it selfish to want to preserve my *own* life? Have you thought about what you're asking of me? To sacrifice myself so that people who can't abide me can live on? And what about me? Will I molder in my grave, remembered only with fear? The selfishness goes both ways, Fion."

"Then what can we do?"

"If you'd thought of that before you'd embraced Tuiloch's lies—"

"Damn you! He used magic. He twisted everything around so that black was white and white was black. How could we know? We're only simple folk, not bloody wizards and shapechangers, used to magic!"

She saw his eyes narrow dangerously and found herself remembering that first morning when he was backed against the wall. Don't shout at him, she told herself. Don't get him angry. Fear skittered through her like a flood of vermin. He could change from man to wolf. He could tear out her throat in less than a—

She stopped the rush of her thoughts with a curse. Arn above! Listen to her. It was just as he said. She couldn't forget what he was now. Could she ever forget? Or would the fear always be there, hidden, but tainting their relationship? And what about Ainsy? Could she lie in his arms without knowing fear, with him being what he was? She was sick with herself, for her thoughts, but the misgivings remained. Shaking her head, she stumbled to her feet, eyes blind with suppressed tears.

"I . . . I'm sorry," she said. "You have as much a right to live as any of us. I didn't mean to demand your help. I. . . ." She wiped her nose on her sleeve, turning her face away from him. "I'll go back."

She took a couple of steps, then turned back. Stram was on his feet, looking from one to the other.

"Kern," Fion said. "I'm sorry. Truly, I am. I know they're just words, but . . . but . . . I was just so scared and I didn't know where to turn."

Her legs felt weak and she trembled so much that she had to lean against a tree to keep her balance. Then Kern was there, supporting her, drawing her close. A moment she hesitated, as another tongue of fear flicked through her, then she folded into his arms like a rag doll.

"I'll come," he said. His own voice was thick with emotion. Awkwardly, he brushed her hair. "I'll help."

She shook her head against his shoulder. "I . . . I didn't realize what I was asking of you. When I left it all . . . all seemed so simple."

"Whisht, Fion. I'm scared too. But I couldn't leave you to him. I know that now. You're my friends. The only ones I've got."

He drew her back and gently held her, rocking back and forth.

"I don't want anybody else to die," she said. "I couldn't stand it. Not you or . . . or anyone. Just him!"

"I'll do my best to keep living for you then," he said, trying to lighten her mood.

He realized that it took less effort than he might have thought. Not five minutes past he'd been wallowing in the depths of depression. Black self-pity from which there'd seemed no chance of escape. But now he knew that he cared—for Fion, for Ainsy, for all of them. And the caring was a strength on its own. Let them live through this trouble and see what the future might bring when it came. And if go he must, at least he would go knowing they still lived.

He wiped Fion's cheeks with the edge of his cloak. "Weep it out," he said "It'll do you good."

His own eyes were shiny with tears. Fion gulped, caught her breath. Slowly the tension eased from her. She let him hold her, pressed against him, and was glad that the fear was only a tiny pinprick far back in her mind. She tried to imagine what it would be like, to be hated and held in such terror, and a new storm of tears threatened to burst forth. Arn above, what a hateful world it could be!

Later they sat apart, though Kern still held her hands between his own.

"The Wolf Moon," Fion said. She spoke softly, as though to herself.

"Mmm?"

"The moon tonight. The first moon of winter's called the Wolf Moon. Maybe it'll bring us luck."

"For my kind," he said, "every moon's a Wolf Moon."

But still he looked up. Though it was no longer in the sky, this time it seemed the moon answered him. It spoke of peace won through effort, earned, not simply given. He squeezed Fion's hands.

"We can use her luck," he said. "And whatever else she's willing to give."

It seemed he heard a sound then, like a wolf's howl, distant and sad, yet holding a promise. Of what he couldn't say. Perhaps it was the wind he heard. Or an echo of his own voice inside his mind. But whatever it was, it comforted him. He saw Stram's ears prick up and felt Fion tense at his side.

"You heard it too?" he asked.

She nodded. "I never believed in her before—not truly.

But I think Arn just answered us. Then again, I never believed in shapechangers before either. Or wizard harpers. . . ."

Kern nodded. He stood and raised her to her feet. "Time we were going," he said.

Fion looked around the cedar shelter. Something in her had changed here—had changed for Kern too. They'd both grown a little wiser, she realized. She felt a sense of loss at leaving the place. It had been a conflicting experience—anger, sorrow, bitterness. But it had offered solace as well, and if not a solution to their problems, at least they'd come somewhat to grips with the meaning of friendship and all it entails. A catharsis, a cleansing. And now, all too soon, the time for action was upon them again.

"His harp's the key," she said as she led the way to her skis.

"I'd thought that as well. With it destroyed, his power's gone. Stripped of it, we'd be dealing with a man as mortal as you or me."

Unless he *was* Yinadral. But that thought, though it visited them both, they left unspoken.

"We should make a plan," Fion said.

"Too soon. Let's first get to the inn and go from there. But I know one thing we'll need."

"What's that?"

"Some clay. Or wax. Either'll do."

"Do for what?"

Kern smiled. "To stop up our ears. How can harpmagic work on us if we can't hear it?"

"There's that," she replied.

"Can you get back to your room before you're missed?"

"I can try. But aren't we going to do something right away?"

"We can't," Kern said. "We don't know how things lie just now. If we wait till, say nightfall, that could give you a chance to try and talk some sense into the others—to break the spell that holds them. Otherwise, Tuiloch could well use them against us."

"Nightfall, then," Fion said.

"Moonrise."

Kern smiled and they both thought of the moon's naming, the first moon of winter, and heard again that sound like wind or a wolf's howl. They stood by the skis. Fion leaned forward and kissed Kern.

"Moonrise it is," she said. "Luck, Kern."

"Luck."

While she buckled on the fastenings of her skis, Kern let his cloak fall to the snow for the last time. He took a deep breath, willed his wolfshape to him, and they were off, the woman followed by the two beasts, wolf and hound. Dawn was pinking the sky by the time they reached the edge of the marshes and soon they saw the outlines of the inn's top story from across the river. Fion knelt by the shore and broke through the ice with one of her poles. Shivering at the water's chill, she worked some clay free. She warmed it under her cloak, then used half on Kern's ears, the other secreted away in a pocket for herself.

"Come away, Stram," she said softly.

She kissed Kern's russet brow, then went on, followed by the dog.

Kern watched them until they reached the barn, then made a circle around the inn buildings, approaching them from the west, through the orchard. With the clay blocking all sound, he moved through an uncanny silence. He never heard the soft scuff of his paws on the ice and snow, or the wind as it clicked the apple boughs together overhead. At the edge of the orchard, he settled down in the snow to watch the inn.

Do you sense me coming, Tuiloch? he asked the new morning. *Are you readying your spells for me? How close will you let me come before you loose your feragh? As far as the inn yard? Or into the inn itself?*

He shrugged. There was only one way to find out. He'd meet with Fion when she had another chance to slip away and they'd form a plan. Until then, he could only watch and wait. And hope.

Fifteenth...

It wasn't until Fion was in her room, stripping off her clothes, that she stopped to think about the trail she'd left. From her window, across the yard to the barn, then the track of her skis heading out into the marshes and returning again. It lay there plain for anyone to see. Shrugging into a warm housecoat, she stood by the window and stared at the sky. Dawn had come, first with the sun, pink to yellow, then followed by a thick overhang of clouds.

Snow! she prayed. Snow, or we're undone before we even begin.

But though the clouds threatened, they held their burden. Biting at her lip, Fion sat down on the edge of her bed and massaged her calves. Last night had been her first time on skis this year and she wasn't accustomed to them yet. She lay back on her bed, listening to the quiet of the inn about her and recalled her conversation with Kern.

Whatever apprehensiveness she'd felt over what he was had been relegated to the back of her mind. Not so much consciously. It had just happened. It must be true, she thought, that a common enemy unites. But before she had time to follow that thought through, the results of yesterday and a sleepless night took their toll and she fell into a deep, dreamless sleep.

She woke to find Ainsy sitting on the end of her bed. Yawning, she wondered how late it was. Then she remembered the trail she'd left and shot a glance out the window. Snow. Blessed Arn, it was snowing! Who said the gods don't listen?

"You're quite the slugabed today," Ainsy said. "You'd think you'd been partying all night or something."

Fion's eyes narrowed and she weighed the tone of Ainsy's words. Almost, this seemed the Ainsy of old—before Tuiloch's coming. Yet how could she be this chipper after all that had happened? That was happening. Tolly's features swam in Fion's mind.

"Ainsy," she said, "what do you remember of yesterday?"

"Remember?" Ainsy's brow furrowed. "It snowed most of the day—as it looks like it will today—and we sat around listening to Tuiloch tell us tales. Why?"

Why? Fion wanted to grab her and shake some sense into her.

"What about Tolly?" she asked.

Her throat constricted with emotion as she spoke his name. Poor Tolly. Slain, and for what? A move in the harper's game. As they might all soon be.

"T-Tolly?"

Ainsy stiffened. She clenched her hands into fists so tightly that her knuckles whitened. "I'd almost forgotten," she said. Her voice was flat and hard. "The wolfman slew him. Butchered him."

Fion reached out to hold her hands. "Not Kern," she said. "It was the harper, Ainsy. It was Tuiloch that killed him, not Kern."

"No!" Ainsy pulled herself free and stood up from the bed. "No! Don't say that! Tuiloch's here to help us. He's all that stands between us and that—that thing."

"Ainsy, please listen to me."

"No! I won't listen to you. What's gotten into you, Fion?"

Fion rubbed her temple. It had been a mistake to bring it up. She saw that now. Ainsy was too bound in the harper's lies to listen to reason.

"You're right," she said, trying to placate Ainsy. It wouldn't do for Tuiloch to hear of what she'd just said. "Of course you're right. I don't know what came over me. I had . . . bad dreams and didn't sleep well."

Ainsy smiled sympathetically and returned to sit on the bed.

"It's the strangeness of it all," she said. "I feel it myself— like there's cobwebs in my head. I forget things. But it'll soon be over. As soon as the snow stops, Tuiloch's promised to hunt that murderer down and we can try to forget the horror."

The horror, Fion thought. And what of the sorrow? Do you feel nothing for Tolly? But she said nothing more to Ainsy of it. She'd been a fool to think she could win through to her. Tuiloch's spells were too powerful.

But if the harper's magics were so strong, why was she still free of his lies? *Was* she even free? What if he knew all along what she and Kern were planning? She remembered Kern telling her of his conversation with the harper. Was Tuiloch only using her where his own words had failed? Did the two of them have a chance, or were they defeated before they ever tried?

She realized that Ainsy had been speaking and set her worries aside with an effort. "What did you say?" she asked.

"I said breakfast's ready. Are you up for some, or do you expect it to be brought up to you?"

Fion managed to find a smile to match the one on Ainsy's lips.

"I'm getting up," she said.

"Well, don't be all day about it!"

Ainsy squeezed Fion's wrist and left the room.

Oh, Arn! Fion buried her face in the pillow. She felt so terribly alone. The thought of getting up and going out to the kitchen, of facing the harper with all she knew and playing through the lies for another day—it all seemed too much for her. But if she didn't. . . If she didn't. . .

Though her every cell and fiber shrank from the task, she knew she must see it through. Composing herself as best as she could, she rose and began to dress. She took the small roll of clay from the inner pocket of her cloak and looked at it for long moments. It was too soon for her to use it. Her hair would hide it well enough, but she still had to be able to hear for now. Later, she promised. She had to remember to wet it down once in a while, that was all. There was only this one more day. She had to play her part.

Hiding the clay in her pocket, she left the room.

Fion felt like a bit player in a mummer's play, suddenly thrust into the main role of a drama on some lord's stage. It was imperative that she maintain her role, yet in the midst of the macabre sense of dislocation that pervaded the inn, she found it hard enough to simply cope, little say playact. The worst of it was that she was the only one to feel this way. There was no one to share the ordeal with. The others were all bound to Tuiloch's will and gave no sign that anything was out of the ordinary.

After her failure at winning Ainsy over, she was hesitant about approaching either Tomtim or Wat. Her gaze shifted constantly to the windows, as unobtrusively as possible, straining hopefully for a glimpse of red fur amid the steady snowfall to buoy up her strength. At the same time she prayed that Kern had enough sense to stay well out of sight.

What she did see through the windows, framed like a white canvas on which an artist had only begun to sketch the outlines of his subject, was the silvery bulk of the feragh. It was almost invisible in the snow, a shadowy shape against the white, only a shade darker than its surroundings, which moved sinuously for its size and set her heart to thumping each time she caught a glimpse of it. There was the feragh, and Tuiloch's eyes that, in her guilt, seemed to follow her every move, waiting for her to give herself away.

It was while they were feeding the livestock, she and Wat and Tomtim, that she tried to get through to the old tinker, only to receive the same blankness that Ainsy had worn, followed by a vehemently expressed hatred for Kern. And like Ainsy, Tolly was no more than a fleeting memory to Tomtim. Tuiloch had successfully driven the stableboy from all their minds. All of them, save Fion.

She changed the subject quickly, before Tomtim got too worked up, and left it at that. It would be useless to try Wat as well. In her heart, she'd expected failure all along anyway. They were on their own, she and Kern.

The snow let up in the late afternoon, though the sky remained overcast. As night drew near, Fion began to fret. Tuiloch never strayed far from his harp and watched her like a hawk. Watched them all, perhaps, but especially her. She hadn't had a chance to sneak out and talk with Kern. What if he was gone? What if he'd slipped away during the day to leave her alone? No! She mustn't think like that. But if she didn't go out to him, what would he be thinking?

Dusk came quickly, the pale daylight leaking darkness until night was suddenly upon them. The sky cleared, glittering stars replacing the cloud overhang. Soon it would be moonrise. Tension bunched in Fion's neck muscles. She felt she should just run off, outside, go to Kern, tell him to call it off, that it was too late, that they were defeated already. Instead, she sat numbly in the common room with the others, waiting. And only she and Tuiloch knew what they waited for.

She fingered the clay in her pocket and wondered when she'd have the chance to stop her ears without any of them seeing what she did. For surely Tuiloch would begin his harping soon. Without protection, she'd become as trapped as the others—wouldn't even remember what she fought for because all reason and will to fight would be washed away with the harper's lies.

The moon rose, and with it came a sound. It shattered the stillness—a long tearing howl of rage and sorrow. The Wolf Moon, Fion thought. But that cry was Kern's. She found the harper's gaze upon her. He smiled wickedly and nodded. Cracking his knuckles—the sound was loud in the sudden silence that followed Kern's cry—he picked up his harp and set it on his lap.

"Now it begins," Tuiloch said.

He drew his fingers along the harpstrings. The notes leaped from the instrument like arrows loosed from a bow, sharp and discordant. Fion clapped her hands over her ears, but the sound carried through the flesh and blood and bone of her hands. Faintly. She heard, but she could fight it. It wasn't strong enough. Tuiloch played louder and the music resounded in Fion's mind. She squeezed her eyes shut to concentrate and willed it away. A greyness like mist came stealing over her, making her thoughts stumble.

"Stop her!" Tuiloch called over the music. "Pull her hands from her ears!"

Ainsy ran to Fion's side and took hold of her hands, trying to force them away from her head. Tomtim and Wat approached. Fion fought Ainsy's grip with all her strength, pulled free, and jumped to her feet. The music was thundering inside her, but she found the will to keep it at bay. Ainsy and the men circled her, hemming her against a wall.

"Please," she said. "Don't. Leave me be."

But there was no recognition in the eyes of the three who stalked her. They were strangers now, made strange by the harpmagic. Even their features seemed transformed, though that was due more to the tears that blurred Fion's sight than any physical mutation. Her back was against the wall now and there was nowhere she could turn. She stared past Ainsy's head to where Tuiloch sat, his fingers tugging painful chords from his harp, his lips twisted with a mocking smile. Then, just as Wat's hand took a grip of her wrist, there came a crash from one of the bedrooms as though a window had been shattered.

For a moment the harpmusic hesitated. Fion tore free from Wat's slack grip and dodged under his arm. Running to the hearth, she grabbed a poker and held it before her. She trembled all over. Her breasts heaved as she drew in ragged breaths. But that moment of being alone against them all had fled.

Kern was here now. Her determination reawakened, hard and sharp inside her, enough to cut through whatever harpmagic Tuiloch might throw at her. Grey and cloying the mists might be, but surely her anger was enough to shear through them?

Sixteenth...

The moon rose and Kern stirred.

He shook the snow from his fur and stared at the inn. Pale moonlight flooded the fields, setting snow crystals glittering. The light seemed to enter him until he felt luminous. Lifting his head, he let loose a howl that tore at the sky. That howl rang across the orchard and fields, but he heard it only dimly in his mind. The clay let in only the sound that carried through the bone of his skull. Unaware of the howl's echoes, he loped forward through a deep silence.

He came in at a run, snow spraying underfoot. He saw the bulky shape of the feragh come quicksilvering toward him, trying to cut him off, but he had too great a lead. Choosing a window, he leaped at it, curling himself into a ball as he struck it. His thick shoulder hair prevented the glass from penetrating deep enough to pierce the skin.

He landed half crouched and skidded across the floor of the darkened room. He could sense the feragh at the window. Its scent was rank and close. The door of the room was ajar and he made for it. Behind him the feragh tore at the window frame to make an opening wide enough to squeeze its bulk through. But before it was even in the room, Kern was through the door and heading down the hall.

He hoped no harm had come to Fion. He'd half expected her not to come to him. Tuiloch would have them all on a close rein by now. He could not afford to do otherwise. Lying out there, waiting, Kern had had more than enough time to think things through. He didn't feel any better about what he did now—at least not in terms of its success—but he'd come to the realization that it was something that must be done. Not even so much for the others, though he did do it for them as well as for himself.

All his life, since that time when his parents had turned against him, he'd been running. It was only now he realized that he'd been running from himself. No matter how far he fled, what he fled from would always be with him, for it was within him, it was himself. In all those years of running, he'd never truly come to grips with what he was.

He'd let himself be cast into the role of the misfit— whether it be among his fellow men or wolves—and never truly tried to rise above it. A life of self-pity had soured and embittered him. But things could change. He had proof of it here, in this very inn. Had Tomtim not realized what he was and kept silent, been willing to trust him and give him the benefit of the doubt? It was not the tinker's fault that Tuiloch had come and seemingly made a mockery of that trust.

No, Kern realized. There *were* people who could accept him for what he was. Other shapechangers, for instance, like the poor girl Tuiloch had boasted of slaying in Jidian. If he survived this night, Kern vowed to seek such folk out, to make a life for himself that was positive instead of being riddled with self-pity and in constant flight. *If* he survived. . . .

He reached the end of the hall and charged into the common room to regard the tableau laid out before him. Ainsy, Wat, and Tomtim stood to his left, dazed, uncertain. By the hearth was Fion with a poker in her hands. And directly in front of him—Tuiloch, harping. Kern's lips split in a wolf grin. He could hear nothing of the music. The harper smiled as well, his fingers on his strings. He opened his mouth and spoke, but he might as well have remained silent for all Kern could hear him.

"The guest of honor arrives," Tuiloch said. He spoke loudly so that his words would carry over the sound of his harping and the noise the feragh was making as he tore at the window. "Yet surely a manshape would be more courteous?"

He tugged the appropriate chords from his harp. His eyes widened slightly when Kern remained as he was. Wolf eyes still burned across the distance that separated them. The wolf grin mocked him as he'd mocked Kern so often before.

To work a spell on a sentient creature, that creature had to be able to hear the spell, hear its true name spoken so that the magic might work. The river clay in Kern's ears effectively blocked any spells that Tuiloch might try. Given the harper's devious mind, his first thought was that somehow Kern had acquired a charm against his harpmagic. A twinge of uneasiness rolled in his stomach as he tried the spell again, this time with more force.

Again nothing.

Tuiloch's fingers faltered on the harp. Watching him, Kern's grin grew wider. He sidled to his right, away from the hallway entrance. From behind he could scent the feragh's approach, the creature's rank smell growing stronger moment by moment. He paused when he had the inn's front door behind him and could watch both the harper and the hallway from where he stood.

He was undecided how to press his attack. Then, as the feragh came into view, Kern's certain knowledge of the situation slipped completely away. All his old fears returned. For a time there, as he leaped ahead of the feragh and won the race to the inn, and later facing down the harper's magic and seeing the consternation spread across Tuiloch's face, elation had come bubbling up in him. He'd stopped to savor the moment, as much as plan what he should do next. He'd come charging in, hoping for inspiration. But inspiration fled at the approach of the feragh.

The color of its pelage seemed to embody the silver that could slay his kind. Like the silver his parents raised against him and the blade thrust in Tuiloch's belt. The sense of strength and purpose that the moonlight had filled him with drained away. Almost he thought he heard harping as well—a vague dissonance that chittered away in the back of his mind. True hearing, or did his memory provide him with that sound?

The feragh paused too, ursine features turned to the harper for direction. Tuiloch thrust a sharp finger in Kern's direction. At the failure of his magic, all desire for subtlety fled him.

"Destroy it!" he roared. "Kill the miserable thing!"

Time seemed to slow. Kern could not hear Tuiloch's command, but he understood its meaning plainly enough. The feragh moved toward him, rose on its hind legs, forepaws prepared to strike. For a moment the inn dissolved around Kern and he thought himself on the ridge once more, the river at his back, the feragh attacking. His shoulder ached in memory of the wound he'd received that day. Then, like a river breaking free of its dam, time moved again, swift as a torrent. He was back in the common room, dodging the feragh's first lightning blows, fighting for purchase on the polished wood floor, seeking the slightest opening that would let him take the offense.

The creature gave him no respite. All eyes were riveted on the unequal combat. But unlike the time on the ridge, Kern was not so weary now. There was no harpmagic sapping the natural strength from his limbs, the sharpness of his reflexes, the savagery of his will. While Tuiloch madly tore chords from his instrument, Kern heard nothing. Not the feragh's roar, not the growls rumbling in his own chest. All his attention was focused on his assailant, narrowed down until only he and it were in the world, battling in some grey nowhere that had no place in the here and now, was in a realm of its own.

But in the common room, events were unfolding.

The sudden appearance of the feragh altered the spell that held Ainsy and the others. Though harpmagic roared on about them, it no longer bound them. Staring with fright-widened eyes at the feragh, understanding descended upon Ainsy with a sickening weight. She fell to her knees as the full import became clear. She knew now what had slain Tolly. Seeing that silver furred monstrosity, how could anyone doubt?

Her glance flickered from it to the harper. Bile arose in her throat. Tolly slain. And by Tuiloch, not Kern. Tuiloch who'd bedded her and—Tolly slain! Tolly dead! She saw the looks of horror on Wat and Tomtim's faces as the same truth struck them. Arn above! How they'd disposed of the body. Tomtim collapsed in shock. A terrible light awoke in Wat's eyes, fueled by a rage so savage that even his dim mind could understand it.

He hurled himself onto the feragh's back, fingers seeking purchase around the creature's muscle-corded throat. A moment's interest the feragh gave him. It shrugged him off, hurling Wat against the wall with a force that knocked the wind from him. As he fell to the floor, his head struck the edge of a chair. A deep gash opened across his forehead, spilling blood into his eyes. Roaring and blind, Wat threw himself at the creature again. This time it turned to meet his attack. The silver claws arced out, raking the big man's chest, flinging him against the wall once more. This time Wat didn't rise.

Kern had not been idle, but the entire episode with Wat had taken mere seconds. He had a mouthful of silver fur and nothing more before the feragh was upon him once more. He twisted out of its grip, spitting hair, dodged a blow, leaped to attack, turning aside at the last moment only to assault it from a new direction. Then he caught a glancing blow from the great paw and went shooting across the room. The creature followed, ready for the kill.

The feragh's appearance had galvanized Fion as well. As Wat went down for the second time, she charged the harper, swinging her poker. Not at Tuiloch did she aim her blow, but at his harp. So intent was he on the battle between feragh and wolf that Tuiloch did not realize her intent until it was too late. The heavy iron poker bit into the instrument, shattering it, stilling its sound forever. But there were uncalled spells stored in its strings and wood, powerful magics that were released in a sudden surge.

Blue fire exploded from the harp. It threw Tuiloch back, singeing his face and chest. But the brunt of the power ran up the poker. Fion screamed. Her hair stood on end. The blue fire crackled along her limbs, burning cold, but not burning, firing her mind with flames of ice that spiraled into an inferno until she could bear no more.

Blessed darkness washed over and she tumbled limply to the floor. The poker fell from her grip with a clatter.

For long moments silence hung. Blue smoke drifted through the common room. Kern stared up into the feragh's hellish eyes, then watched it slowly dissolve. In the heat of battle, some of the brittle clay in his ears had broken free, but all he heard was a dull roar in his ears. He could scarcely move. His left foreleg was broken at the shoulder. Some ribs, too, were broken, or cracked. Yet. . . . He could hardly believe it. They had won. Against all odds, they had won!

He took manshape then, gasping as the pain hit him with renewed fury. Every breath was an effort, every motion an agony, but he raised himself with his good arm so that he was leaning against the wall. They'd won, but at what cost? He saw Fion lying in a pitiful sprawl and his joy became a bleak well of sorrow. He looked around the room—took in Wat's limp bulk, Tomtim untouched, but stunned with shock, and Ainsy dull-eyed and white. But time and again his gaze returned to where Fion lay. Cursing the pain that came with the slightest motion, he began to haul himself along the floor to her side.

Don't be dead, he pleaded. Stars and moon, I beg you, don't let her be dead.

But he never reached her side.

Shaking his head, Tuiloch arose. He stood like a giant in his anger as he pulled the silver blade from his belt. In helpless rage, Kern watched him approach. He tried to will his wolfshape back to him, but the pain clouded his mind too much to concentrate.

"For . . . for what you have done this night," Tuiloch said, "I will not give you an easy death. For slaying my brother. . . ."

Kern understood. The feragh was bound to the harp. When Fion had destroyed the instrument, she'd destroyed the monster with it. Yet deadly though the silver blade in his hand might be, Tuiloch was only a man now, the same as Kern. His magics were gone, fragmented with the shards of wood and twisted strings his instrument had become. If Kern could only raise himself up . . . meet this attack.

Tuiloch's eyes glittered with power.

"Fool!" he said bitterly. "Did you think the harp my power? Music is my power! The harp only stored my spells, housed my brother. The brother you slayed!"

He began to hum and the sound filled the room. Magic crackled in the air, leaped like sparks from the harper's blade. Kern had half raised himself from the floor. Now grey tendrils of mist came snaking into his mind and he fell back to the floor. Helplessly, he watched Tuiloch approach.

Fight it, he demanded of himself. Fight it!

But the mists thickened and stuck to his thoughts, dulling his will. They clotted inside him, each new tendril joined to others until no matter how tenaciously he fought them, he could do nothing. The silver blade winked in the candlelight that lit the room. The light sped up and down its edge and Kern could only stare fascinated at it as he waited for the blow that must follow. And deep inside, where what remained of his will huddled against Tuiloch's power, he railed against the unfairness of it. That Fion should have given herself up for nothing. That it must end like this.

He tried again. He stared at the knife blade, used it as a focus while he tried to free himself of the yoke of Tuiloch's spell. The sound that came from between the harper's lips resembled nothing human. It was harping, but harping that was never born of harpstrings. It sounded like a multitude of instruments, all rolled into one, playing a hellish dissonant music that carried only death in its notes. Kern's death. On that blade's edge. Silver.

Then the blade was gone. The music had stopped.

Not understanding what had happened, Kern still seized his opportunity. He snapped his will into a blade as sharp as Tuiloch's knife and cut himself free of the clotted mists that fogged his mind. He called up his wolf-shape, for in that form he could withstand pain more than he could as a man. Fighting his way to his feet, ignoring as best he could the sharp spasm that came with each breath, he saw what had stayed the harper's hand. Ainsy.

She'd jumped on his back, knocking him to the floor, then grabbed for the knife hand. But the harper's strength was too much for her. He didn't need to resume his humming to defeat her. He hit her once across the face. Then again. Her grip faltered on his arm and he pulled free, smashing her to the floor with a third blow. As the blade meant for Kern leaped for her heart, the wolf threw himself into the struggle.

With one leg useless, his attack didn't have much force behind it. But it was enough for his jaws to reach the harper's arm. They snapped on his wrist, shattering bone, tearing muscle. Tuiloch screamed and the knife fell to the floor. He struck Kern about the muzzle until the wolf had to let go.

They backed off from each other, Kern throbbing with pain, the harper nursing his mangled wrist with his good hand, hatred howling in his eyes. Tuiloch tried to resume his magic, but now he was the one who couldn't concentrate clearly enough. The humming that came from between his lips was disjointed, without the assurance behind it on which magic thrived.

Kern readied himself for the kill. He let his mind fill with all the horrors for which Tuiloch was responsible, until he trembled with cold anger. Killing anger. Then he felt a hand tug at his shoulder hairs, a voice in his ear.

"K-Kern. No."

He couldn't believe what he'd heard. Surely the residual clay in his ears was distorting her words? After all Tuiloch had done, she couldn't mean to let him live? He'd only go off to mend his wounds and return for vengeance. He turned to look at her. He'd never seen her through wolf eyes before, save for those hectic moments just past. Her face seemed thinner from this new perspective, but it was still the face of the woman he loved. He could see past the shock and tenseness and still see her as she'd been before all this had begun. But she was lost to him now. He'd never see that face again. And she expected him to let the perpetrator of that crime live? Of that crime and so many others, so much worse?

"If I saw you . . . kill him like . . . like that . . . I could never forget it, Kern. Never. No matter . . . how hard I tried."

What was she saying? What did it matter if she could never forget it? She could balance that memory against Tolly being slain—Tolly and Fion and Wat—and at least know that justice had been done, even if the dead couldn't be returned. Wasn't that better than to let the harper go free? He would only kill again. Build a new harp. Wreak his vengeance on them and continue with his killing. Sweet stars! What if he *was* Yinadral? How many deaths was he responsible for?

He took back his manshape to explain this to her. In that moment Tuiloch, forgotten by Kern, struck again. He knocked Kern down and scrabbled for the blade. But Kern's hand reached it first. He thought he'd faint from the pain. Thought he'd never get his fingers to keep their grip on the knife's hilt. It was slippery to the touch, wet with fear-induced sweat.

Tuiloch thrust his crushed wrist into Kern's face, blinding him with blood, and lunged for the knife hand. Kern twisted. Where he found the strength, he never knew. But he threw the harper from him and the blade flashed high, then down. Once. Twice. His hand slipped on the leather hilt and touched the silver of the blade. It burned like no pain he'd felt before. He fell back, nursing his hand, trying to concentrate on Tuiloch, on the harper's next move. But that move never came.

Slowly Kern wiped the blood from his eyes and stared down at his nemesis. The blade thrust up from Tuiloch's chest and his face was so contorted that it seemed a stranger's. In death, Tuiloch's features had a withered look to them. The handsomeness that Kern remembered had dissolved into what seemed more like some gaunt bird of prey.

Feeling sick, Kern turned away. His head spun. His stomach roiled with an acidic burning sensation. Pain throbbed in his chest and shoulder, fired through his hand.

Then he felt a touch on him—a gentle touch, holding him, caressing him. Unwilling to believe, he forced his eyes open, fought the pain to focus on a face six inches from his own. Ainsy. Ah, Ainsy. If it could only be. . . . He shook his head and tried to pull away, but she held him tighter. He looked, saw the love in her eyes, the trembling of her lips, and couldn't understand.

"Can . . . can you forgive me?" she asked.

"Forgive *you?* For what?"

"For not believing in you. For believing in lies. What I've done. . . ." She shuddered. "And still you cared enough to come back and help us."

Kern wanted to lie now, to say it was all right and let things somehow return to how they'd been before. But he was done with lies. "I *am* a shapechanger," he said slowly. The words were difficult, but once started, the rest came more easily. Like a weight lifting from his heart. "That was no lie of Tuiloch's. I am what he said I was."

"I know."

"Then . . . ?"

"But you're not what he said you were," she explained. "A shapechanger, yes. But not a killer. I can't believe it. I've not known you long, Kern, but I know your kindness and gentle ways. We've been too close and I love you too much to believe you're anything evil. You can't be!"

"I brought all . . . all this to you, didn't I?"

Ainsy shook her head fiercely. "No! He did. Tuiloch. Not you. Don't ever say that."

Kern could only stare at her. He still found it hard to believe what he was hearing her say. He'd heard of moments like this. Shock, a time of stress. It left people open, vulnerable. When the weakness passed, how would she react then? But he knew Ainsy well enough to know that she wasn't lying, not even to herself.

"We . . . we'll talk . . . later," he said. "I. . . ."

He was finding it hard to concentrate. Everything was a blur. A part of him leaped for joy at her words. But he remembered Tolly and the farmer. And Fion and Wat. Were they dead? And if not, how bad were their hurts? What of Tomtim? Who lived and who had died? But he couldn't connect his thoughts to his voice.

Her face swam in his vision and suddenly he saw no more. Only an endless darkness into which he was falling. He fought the sensation for as long as he could, but he was too weak to hold out for long. He let the darkness claim him.

They all recovered in time, save the harper.

Tomtim, ashamed of the feeble part he'd played in their deliverance, took the sleigh into Hay-on-Pen and fetched back a healer. Her name was Telina and she was a stern old dame, well into her sixties, given to a brusque manner, plain clothes, and her hair pulled severely back from her face. But her hands were gentle and she knew her calling better than most. She rode back to the inn without complaint, as soon as Tomtim began his tale, and stayed on until the last of her charges seemed well on the way to recovery.

For Kern and Wat it was simply a matter of setting

bones straight and cleaning the blood from their wounds before binding them. She clucked to herself as she sewed stitches in Wat's brow, but assured Ainsy that the big man would be on his feet soon enough. She had an ointment for Kern's hand that helped to heal the silverburn quickly, though it left a scar both in manshape and wolf's.

Fion was another matter. She lay in a coma for almost a week and, even just before she woke, Telina could not be certain that she ever would.

"Magic you say?" she'd muttered. "Don't know magic. She's in Arn's hands, this one is. All we can do for her is pray."

It seemed that their prayers did some good. Kern, despite his own wounds—and both Ainsy and Telina's scoldings—kept a vigil by her bed. He was alone with her when she woke and, looking into her clearing eyes as they opened, finally felt it had all been worthwhile.

"Kern?"

"I'm here."

He knew he should call the others, but she reached for him weakly, wincing with the movement. She looked at her hand strangely, taking in the bandages. It was the only physical harm she'd taken from the harp's blue fire, from the backlash of magic. Both her hands were badly burned. But they were mending.

"We . . . we won, didn't we?"

Kern nodded. His eyes were damp with emotion. "You won for us, Fion. We all did what we could, but without you, we'd all be lying there dead and the harper would have gone free. You're a brave lass and there's no mistaking it."

Fion smiled. "I never knew what would happen," she said. "Never thought there'd be that reaction. It was like being swallowed by blue fire. I seemed to drift in a place of nothingness for so long. . . ."

She shivered, remembering.

"Don't think of it," Kern said.

"I'll try not to. Kern. What about Ainsy?"

"She wants me to stay."

"And will you?"

"What do you think?"

Her smile grew wider and she closed her eyes with a self-satisfied air. Leaning forward, Kern kissed her lightly on the brow, then went to call the others.

Last...

It was late spring. The nights were still chilly, but there was green on the trees and in the fields, and everyone knew that winter was finally on its way out.

Kern stepped from the inn and softly closed the door behind him. Above, the moon was just reaching its apex. From across the river came the cries of night birds and bullfrogs, and once the lonely bellow of a moose. Kern smiled. It was a good night for a run.

Carefully he took off his clothes and laid them on the flagstones by the door. Then he fastened a keg about his neck with a leather loop. Preparations done, he took on his wolfshape and loped out of the inn yard, heading over the bridge. The keg bounced against his chest, but the weight didn't bother him. He was too filled with the moon and stars, the scents that rode the wind, the grass underfoot when he left the bridge.

He paused on the far side and looked back. Squinting, he could just make out the tall stone that marked Tolly's grave. They'd never recovered his body, but they'd raised the marker so that his spirit would know that they hadn't forgotten him. And the harper? They'd given him a murderer's death—burned him in the woods with the remnants of his instrument. He they'd almost forgotten. He was never spoken of, though Kern knew that Ainsy still had nightmares about him from time to time.

He shrugged and set off. He still had a good deal of his winter's coat and looked a little shaggy with the shedding hair in among the rest. He wondered if he could convince Wat to give him a brushing tomorrow. The big man certainly brushed Stram often enough.

His shapechanging was the inn's secret. They all knew about it, but none of them would ever speak of it to an outsider. Kern had wanted to attempt to put aside that part of himself, but the others would have none of it.

"It'd be unnatural," Tomtim had said. "For you, leastways."

"It's not a curse," Ainsy had added. "You can't ever think that. It's the way you are."

The way he was. He thought back to the wolf who'd entered this valley last autumn and couldn't recognize him. He could never thank Tuiloch for driving him to the inn, though in the long run the harper had been responsible. Tuiloch. *Was* he Yinadral? He doubted that they would ever truly know. But there were others he could thank. Like the kimeyn. Who else could it have been but they who brought him to the inn?

He'd caught their scent more than once on a night

jaunt and knew they watched the inn the odd time. After a long serious discussion with Wat, the two of them decided that one good turn deserved another. And, knowing their fondness for the ale Ainsy brewed in the Tinker's cellar, what better to offer them than a keg of it?

He knew a place where they came to from time to tune. An old oak tree—a "moon-oak" Tomtim had called it when Kern described it to him. The name came from the loop in one of its branches that was shaped like a crescent moon. Fion insisted it was called a "kissing-oak," for there the woodsmen had their revels.

He reached the tree before midnight and changed briefly to a man—only long enough to undo the leather ties and set the keg in a crook of the oak's roots. They'd find it there. And others he'd leave once in a while. It was little enough in return for their taking him to the inn when he was hurt. They'd appreciate it and, besides, it was better than having them steal it.

Kern chuckled. He looked up into the tree, traced the crescent shape with his gaze. Lifting his head, he loosed a long joyous howl—to the night, to the moon, to his new life. Then he bounded away into the woods for his run. He'd not stay long. Ainsy was waiting for him back home. Home. What a ring that word had to it. She'd be asleep, but she'd wake quick enough when she felt him getting into bed.

Thinking of her brought him to an abrupt halt. To the winds with a run tonight. He turned and made for the inn.